"You are ruthless enough for anything!"

Emma's accusation was blatant.

"You're right—I am ruthless," Nicholas agreed. "I know what I want, Emma, and yes, I'm ruthless enough to get it. But what about you? You want to stay on at Whitewayes. Are you prepared to go to any length?"

She nodded. "Yes."

"Then may I suggest, dear Emma, that you marry me?"

"You're joking!" she managed to breathe.

"I never joke," he responded quietly.

"You're crazy, then." Emma collapsed into a chair. What choice did she have? She was so tired of fighting. She wanted to stay at Whitewayes, true, but that wasn't all she wanted from Nicholas Voss. She couldn't really predict what this marriage was going to accomplish—but suddenly she knew what her answer must be....

Fool's Paradise

by

ANN COOPER

Harlequin Books

TORONTO • LONDON • LOS ANGELES • AMSTERDAM
SYDNEY • HAMBURG • PARIS • STOCKHOLM • ATHENS • TOKYO

Original hardcover edition published in 1980
by Mills & Boon Limited

ISBN 0-373-02383-9

Harlequin edition published February 1981

Printed in U.S.A.

CHAPTER ONE

'*Nicholas Voss!*' Emma swished together the long velvet curtains and turned back to the bearer of such news. 'Why, of all people,' she exclaimed, 'did they have to choose *him*?'

Uncle Louis crossed one elegant leg over the other, twitched his grey Vandyck beard uncertainly, and gazed at her from the deep chintz-covered settee.

'It was a unanimous decision, my dear,' he began, with a characteristic shrug. 'The Trustees obviously believe he's the best man for the job.'

Emma snorted and marched over to the fire, picking up the brass poker and bending to give vent to her fury on the blazing logs. Her dark cap of sleek hair shone in the firelight and amber eyes gleamed like the reflected sparks she was staring at.

Nicholas Voss! She saw his sardonic face momentarily etched in the black soot at the back of the fire. This was the man she had vowed to hate for the rest of her life; the tormentor of her dreams. And he was coming here, to Whitewayes. What on earth would that mean?

She rocked back on her heels and gazed at the dancing flames, memories of five years ago returning as vividly as if they had happened only yesterday. She saw a carefree girl of eighteen, a dashing sophisticated man, who even then had been approaching thirty. And he had swept Emma headlong into a whirlwind summer. Long, warm days – longer nights. The scent of roses ... and the sea. All memories she thought had disappeared into the back of her mind, but now, at the unexpected mention of his name, everything paraded before her imagination with violent intensity.

'They couldn't really have chosen you, Emma.' Uncle Louis' gentle voice cleared her mind. 'You know I can't stay on here indefinitely,' he continued, when she turned to gaze up at him from the rug. 'And you couldn't have managed alone.' His expression stopped the hasty retort that sprang to her lips. 'You know I don't mean that you couldn't cope with it all. I'm sure you could run Whitewayes as well as anyone,' he assured her diplomatically. 'But it would soon become common knowledge that there was a woman here, living alone ... and with so many treasures ...' He trailed to silence and Emma had to acknowledge the sense of something she had really known herself all along. 'You couldn't expect the committee to take such a decision, however they might feel personally – as you were Gilbert's daughter ...' This time the silence was deeper as they both remembered Emma's father who had made Whitewayes his life – before his tragic and untimely death.

Emma sighed, and patted her uncle's knee affectionately. 'Daddy wanted everything to stay the same,' she began. It still wasn't easy to talk of the father to whom she had been so close. 'I promised him I'd carry on. I know his ways – what he would have wanted,' she added firmly, and for a moment her huge eyes seemed even larger in her pale, elfin face.

'Nicholas *is* a member of the family,' Louis reminded her gently. 'Even if his lineage is somewhat distant.'

'Distant!' Emma retorted, scrabbling to her feet and sinking into a chair on the other side of the graceful Adam fireplace. 'You can't get much more distant than he is. He hasn't been near here – hasn't shown the slightest interest in the place.' Her eyes slid away from her uncle's. Perhaps there was a good reason for Nicholas' absence. He probably had no wish to see Emma again, either.

'Of course,' Uncle Louis began after a few moments, 'the Trustees would have preferred a married man. So much more – stable,' he suggested, after carefully searching for the right word.

Married! Nicholas Voss married? No! The sense of Louis' words filtered through her sudden panic. But images were leaping again ... A cabin cruiser

moored by a jetty ... 'Marry me, Emma – marry
me ...' The words had echoed down the years,
full of laughter and scorn, and she saw herself
running away from him, soft deck-shoes making
no sound as she had raced along the slatted boards.
Away – away from Nicholas and out of his life
for ever.

'That's why I suggested that you remain here –
as his assistant,' Louis continued. His tone was
soothing now. Did he realise Emma's turmoil?
How much did he know of that affair five summers
ago? She smiled across at him, this her favourite
uncle, her mother's brother; a mother she had
never known. There had seemed to be only her
father and Louis for as long as she could remember.
But Uncle Louis was far happier in his bachelor
state in London. 'I'm set in my ways,' he had said,
after her father's fatal illness. 'But of course I'll
stay on with you at Whitewayes, until things get
sorted out.'

And this was the sorting out, thought Emma, her
eyes lovingly travelling around the room with its
lofty ceiling, delicate plasterwork and tall double
doors. Space and timeless elegance. But it was also
warm and cosy and the only home she had, and it
didn't matter if the small park outside was visited
by lonely old ladies who came to feed the ducks, or
if young lovers walked hand in hand in the copse
or gazed at the lake – or wandered over the major-

ity of the house. Part of it belonged to Emma. And if it wasn't the bricks and mortar, then maybe she had inherited the spirit of the place. Whitewayes – a long white house, as the name suggested, which could no longer be filled with the happy laughter of a boisterous family – so it opened its doors with a dignified indulgence to the boisterous ramblings of many families.

'Nicholas' assistant?' Had Louis been dropping off to sleep? His head jerked as Emma looked back at him. 'Has he agreed to have me?'

'I've no idea.' He sipped his sherry, savouring the pleasure with a little ritual play-acting, and Emma was instantly alert. Uncle Louis was up to something. He had his vague, everything's-quite-beyond-me-these-days look, which he used as a disguise when he was about to be particularly devious.

'Perhaps Nicholas Voss won't want me as his assistant,' Emma said firmly. 'Maybe I won't want to stay.'

Her uncle's sharp eyes flew to her face, then they returned to the lazy contemplation of his sherry glass. He twisted the stem, playing tricks with firelight and crystal. 'I think Gilbert would have wanted you to stay,' he almost whispered, and the quiet words set a seal on Emma's dilemma.

She had to stay, to see this thing through. Even if it was only to stop Nicholas Voss running roughshod over her beloved home.

It was a pity, she thought, that the family had long since relinquished their hold of a property which had financially become impossible to keep. But, fortunately, certain conditions had been made with the beginning of the trust, and one of those conditions was that a member of the family should always be appointed custodian.

Unfortunately, Emma was convinced that the latest member of the family to be appointed was going to change everything her father had worked for. Wasn't it bad enough that she had only Uncle Louis' spasmodic support. Now she had to contend with this ruthless business man, who would see Whitewayes as a balance sheet instead of a gracious, if somewhat small, stately home.

Such thoughts were not conducive to peaceful slumber. Emma tossed and turned for most of the night and some instinct had her up the next morning, and out of the house just as a grey dawn was streaking the sky. The January morning was damp, unusually mild for the time of year; spring bulbs were already protruding.

In an old mac and headscarf, she wandered along gravel paths, down worn and cracking steps and beneath trees that showered her when the damp breeze ruffled their bare branches. It was so peaceful, as yet too early for the distant roar of London's traffic to reach way up here. But beneath the peace Emma had the uncomfortable and lost feeling that this was the end of an era. How long would Nicholas Voss tolerate her presence at Whitewayes? Soon she might be quite homeless. And to lose all this ... Standing down by the lake, she sighed and looked back at the elegant white house with its tall windows, wide terrace and ornamental flower beds. A gently sloping, wide expanse of lawn rose between her and the house her family had loved for generations, and suddenly, in that moment, she knew she wasn't submitting to the Trustees' decision without a fight. If Nicholas Voss had to come here she couldn't stop him. But she would do everything – or anything – in her power to prevent him obtaining total control.

It was beginning to drizzle, so Emma said goodbye to the ducks and hurried back towards shelter, taking a short cut across the small forecourt before heading towards a side door. And then she saw it; a low, sleek, sporty Daimler which had been conspicuously parked near the front entrance.

Couldn't they read the notice which said the house wouldn't be open until ten o'clock? Emma looked at her watch. Barely eight-fifteen. Who would be visiting them at such an ungodly hour?

She practically ran round to the side door and let herself in. Two steps took her out of the narrow passage and into the spacious hallway. All was silent. Uncle Louis would be hardly out of bed. Who had let in the stranger? Emma's heart stood still. Or maybe it wasn't a stranger. Maybe it was ... She compressed her lips angrily. If it was Nicholas Voss he certainly didn't believe in wasting time!

She threw her damp mac and scarf over the banister and tugged at the ribbing of her faded pink sweater. 'And I'm wearing this old skirt,' she thought irritably, 'and my hose are probably splashed with mud.' But what did it matter how she looked? This wasn't the old days ... and she slowly crossed to the double doors marked 'Private' before stretching out an unsteady hand. Five years – it was a long time. How did you say hullo to a man you had once loved?

Hesitantly she went inside and refastened the door with extra special care, keeping her eyes lowered, as she had since entering the room. For the first time in her life she was conscious of breathing; it necessitated inhaling and exhaling with supreme control. The door was eventually closed and she was obliged to turn and face the dimly lit room.

'Good morning, Emma.' Nicholas Voss stood in the patriarchal position; hands clasped behind him – back to the fire. His firm bass voice was exactly as she remembered, but he looked different. There was five years of difference – five years of *living* – in the enigmatic eyes and sensuous face.

But it seemed some things didn't change in five years. As they stood, the length of the room apart, Emma felt as close to Nicholas as if he had been touching her. It had always been the same; this tight, invisible cord of emotion binding them together.

Uncertainly she walked towards him, testing her responses as of old, and suddenly she felt the utter hopelessness of realising she still loved him as desperately as before.

Time – separation – weren't they supposed to heal all things? Emma could feel the old agony returning, the sharp twist in her heart at losing him, and she knew the wound was as deep as ever – nothing had healed.

'It's been a long time,' said Nicholas quietly. His voice was expressionless, yet now there was a keenness about his eyes which he didn't attempt to disguise.

Emma knew he was looking for the slightest sign of the very emotion which threatened to overwhelm her. Self-control wasn't easy to find – but somehow she managed it.

'It must be four – or is it *five* years?' she began. 'I remember you used to call me Pixie. How long ago all that seems now,' she added, giving a hollow little laugh. The words had come perfectly, as if she had been a well-rehearsed actress; but there was no applause.

Nicholas Voss gazed at her for five long, excruciating seconds, then his lips slowly parted to reveal gleaming white teeth.

'I see we understand each other perfectly,' he said, in a new, clipped voice. 'You've greatly matured, Emma, since we last met.'

Her deception had worked. She felt relieved – and desperate. Had she been expecting him to make some declaration of his own? 'Yes, it's been a long time, Emma, but we're together again now, and that's all that matters.' But of course he didn't say it. How foolish even to contemplate such an idea!

'Of course I've changed. A lot can happen in five years,' she said simply, going over to the french windows and pulling back the curtains. It was raining quite steadily now; the park looked damp, grey and desolate.

'I'm sorry for the circumstances which bring us together now,' he went on, his voice returning to normal.

Sorry! Nicholas Voss didn't have room in his heart to be sorry for anyone. She turned sharply from the window.

'You weren't at the funeral.'

'I was in America – I didn't get the news ... But I wrote.'

She shrugged. 'There were a lot of letters.'

'Gilbert was well loved,' he began.

She had no intention of discussing her father with this man, and while her mind searched for a suitable reply he studied her carefully.

If I have changed, thought Emma, then so has he, more than I'd first noticed. There was a hardness about his eyes that hadn't been there before, a sort of world-weariness which emphasised the sophisticated aura which hung about him. Nicholas Voss had always been an attractive, vital man and five years had certainly enhanced that image. But now Emma could sense something new in the atmosphere, something sharp and brittle ... It made him almost a stranger.

'I assume Louis has told you that I shall be taking over ...'

'He's explained everything — perfectly,' she interrupted, moving restlessly from window to window, aware of his eyes following her as she opened all the curtains. The simple action momentarily relieved her nerves, but she could have done without the misty light creeping into the room. Now she could see the deep, unfathomable blue of Nicholas' eyes, as if a black and white film had suddenly turned to Technicolor. It accentuated his fresh skin and the determined outline of his jaw. It was a determination she knew she would have to battle against. The thought was not comforting.

'I didn't expect you to come quite so quickly,'

she said at last. 'You must have been very anxious to make a start.'

He was annoyed by her inference, exactly as she had intended. His lips thinned. 'I'm on my way north – a sale in Derbyshire. I just called in to say hullo – to see how things were.'

'With me – or with the house?' Emma asked, waving a hand around the room. 'Do you approve of what you see? Have we been looking after the place? I trust you have an inventory. Do you want to check everything now?' She swallowed and tried to keep her chin raised, but it wasn't easy. Instinctively she realised she had gone too far.

'I don't think that will be necessary.' His eyes opened wide with anger, and the effort of controlling it. She could feel his rage leaping towards her. Then it was gone, instantly, and a man of ice and hardness stood before her. 'It will take a little while to organise my other business commitments,' he began, 'a week or two, perhaps. I'm quite sure you and Louis will carry on admirably till then.' His face should have been enough to render her silent, but she was out of practice in dealing with this man – nerves made her voluble.

'Of course we can manage – we've managed perfectly well up till now without your ...' she had been about to say 'interference', but Nicholas' sharp exclamation finally stopped her.

He threw back his head and gave a brief, contemptuous laugh. 'But you have *not* managed perfectly well, Emma. Not since Gilbert's death – in fact,' he went on seriously, after only the slightest hesitation, 'in fact, not for the past five years. Unfortunately, your father was not a business man. The situation is quite serious, I assure you.'

'How *dare* you accuse us ...' she blurted, all thought of what Nicholas Voss had been to her instantly vanishing as she rushed to the defence of her father. 'He spent the last ten years of his life *loving* this place ...'

'But *loving* isn't enough, is it?' was Nicholas' quick response. 'You can't pull resources out of thin air. They have to be planned for – worked at...'

'Are you suggesting we haven't *worked* – haven't nearly dropped with exhaustion at times? This isn't a big estate, I know,' Emma admitted, 'but it's quite big enough for two people to run. Have you any idea of the organisation needed? Of the hundred and one things that go wrong every day? ...' Her voice had become shrill – uncontrollable; Nicholas Voss strode towards her.

'Emma – stop it!' He shook her by the shoulders. 'I had no intention of discussing the matter today. It's all far too soon, but changes will have to be made. It's unavoidable, I'm afraid. It should have been done years ago.'

'What should?' Emma wrenched herself out of

his grasp and took a pace or two backwards. 'What should have been done?' she repeated. It sounded as if he had everything planned.

'I really haven't time.' He glanced at the Napoleon ormolu clock on the mantelpiece. 'The motorway will be dreadful in this weather. I really had intended leaving town by eight-thirty.'

'I don't think it will take you long to explain your ideas,' Emma almost whispered. She had retreated behind the sofa, leaning against its tall back. It was a support – a barricade, something of a comfort.

'If you insist.' He shook his head slightly, not caring if she disliked what he was about to say. He probably thought she would have to find out sooner or later anyway. 'We have to make this house pay for itself,' he began.

'Impossible,' she said briefly.

'Maybe, but let's say our bank account has to be less in the red.'

'You're not selling one painting, or piece of porcelain, or one stick of furniture, if that's what you have in mind.'

'No, Emma,' he began wearily, 'it isn't what I have in mind. We couldn't sell them, anyway. We don't have the authority.'

'What, then?' Angry eyes, the colour of topaz, glared at him.

'I intend making those articles you've mentioned

earn their own keep. Some people are really interested, as we are; I don't mean the casual visitor
wandering around, I mean the person who is prepared to spend time – and money,' he added firmly,
'learning and discussing works of art.'

Emma felt the beginnings of an idea creep into
her mind. He couldn't – he wasn't really ... But
this time she remained silent and waited for him
to continue.

'So I've asked around, got a few people interested,' he went on. 'I don't think it would take
us long to organise residential courses for – say –
twenty people at a time. Maybe more if we could
cope. We'll have to see.'

It was exactly as she had imagined. The idea was
appalling. 'You're out of your mind,' she said
fiercely.

'No, Emma – I'm *not*.' His strong voice carried
with it absolute determination. 'If we don't make
a concerted effort to alter the financial problems of
this establishment, then the family will lose its
tenuous grasp. One of the big Trusts will move in,
and you and I won't even be allowed to stay here –
much less have a say in what happens to Whitewayes.'

'My father didn't work the last ten years of his
life to have that happen.' Tears choked her – of
rage or desperation, she wasn't sure.

His eyes flashed dangerously. 'And I have no

intention of losing this place, Emma. Whatever the cost to either of us. Personal feelings don't count.'

'I think you're making a very big mistake,' she managed to say, as he picked up his briefcase and obviously prepared to depart.

As he passed the back of the sofa he paused, looking down at her, and for a second a certain light flickered across his eyes. A muscle down the side of his stern face jerked as he came nearer and took her chin in a firm grasp.

'That's where you're wrong,' he said icily. 'This time I know *exactly* what I'm doing. Five years ago – that's when I made my mistake!'

CHAPTER TWO

MISTAKE? What mistake? The mistake of loving her – or losing her? But Emma couldn't ask, and Nicholas was in no mood to elaborate. His fingers on her chin increased their pressure and the build-up of tension stretched between them. The silence grew thicker – menacing – the only audible sound being the delicate tick from the mantelpiece. Emma felt threatened, overwhelmed, as much by the physical dominance of this man as by the problems he presented for Whitewayes. Her own responses to him were undeniable. She wanted him – as much as ever – and couldn't he tell? By the way her body rocked against him, by the faint tinge of warm colour creeping to her cheeks. He had seen it all before, her gradual arousal to desire – which he had manipulated expertly time and time again. Only then, five years ago, there had been desire matched with desire; hers and Nicholas'. And the ignition of those days was still to be remembered as she drew inextricably closer to him.

But now he discarded her without preamble, just an unconscious shrug and a careless flick of his wrist, and the separation was complete. It was obvious that he hadn't suffered from the same agonising memory of the past. His eyes were unwavering as they steadfastly regarded her.

'Maybe you haven't changed as much as I'd first imagined,' he said, with a curious twist to his mouth. Emma was appalled. So he *had* noticed. Now he knew exactly how she felt about him – and the idea amused him, intrigued him almost. She could see the new possibilities presenting themselves to his heightened imagination. 'I think we may find working together quite – interesting,' he said after a few moments. 'Think about what I've said, Emma. Maybe you can come up with a few suggestions of your own.'

'The only suggestion I'd like to make is …' Anger made her speak hastily, but she only got that far.

'I can imagine,' came the quick reply. 'But don't delude yourself,' he taunted. 'You don't really want me to disappear into thin air – you only *think* you do.'

'I have absolutely no idea what you're talking about,' Emma defended.

'You haven't?' There was a hint of mockery wrapped up in his words. 'Come, come, Emma, this isn't like you. You always used to know exactly what I was talking about.' He came a pace or two nearer and Emma backed off. Her heel caught on the edge of a rug and she slipped on the shining parquet. Nicholas caught her, gently this time, the hand on her arm inviting, sensuous, his blue eyes now leaping and darting with devilment. 'Let's see what else you think you don't want,' he practically purred, and before she could stop him, he tossed his briefcase into a chair and pulled her roughly into his arms.

In the second she didn't resist she heard him laugh, a strong, vibrant but harsh sound that made her look up at him in horror. This wasn't the man who had captured her love, had nurtured it, allowed it to blossom, fed it with gentleness and understanding. This was the monster who had nearly drawn from her the completeness of love. When she had been almost ready to surrender totally, he had tried to influence her decision by a worthless proposal. 'Marry me, Emma.' She shuddered at the memory. He might just as well have said, 'Sleep with me, Emma.' And if she had? All those years ago in a tiny cabin-cruiser, what would have been the outcome today? At least she still had self-respect on her side. Nicholas hadn't liked losing then, and it appeared he carried the bitterness of rejection right up to the present day.

Now, with his arms tightly around her, a firm hand exploring her back and bringing her magically alive, Emma knew that Nicholas hadn't slept easy for five years, either. Only his thoughts were those of revenge. Five years had turned Nicholas Voss into a ruthless, demanding tyrant.

She struggled to break free, but the taut muscles and strong, powerful limbs pressed tightly against her, and it was humiliating to be unable to move one inch.

'You always were a little minx,' he whispered huskily, grabbing a handful of hair and forcing her head backwards. 'But I always knew the remedy for all your nonsense.' Emma recognised the imperceptible alteration of his features, the flaring of his nostrils, the smoothing from his face of every emotion save that of desire, the sensuous lips held firmly together. It was his pattern – his prelude to love.

To be kissed was unavoidable, but it was the kiss of a stranger – hard, ruthless, a rough attack on sensibilities. There was no love, no tenderness, just passion – and punishment. But it was exciting – stimulating, and Emma found herself responding with equal kind, hungry for him in whatever manner he chose to allow.

It couldn't have lasted long, half a minute, no more, yet when he pushed her from him Emma felt she had lived more completely than in all the five years put together. He was breathing hard, staring at her curiously, so she stared back, the soft pink sweater rising and falling as she endeavoured to bring some control to her emotions.

'My, my, you have been a busy girl,' he said after a while, strolling across to the chair and collecting his case. Then he turned round and added almost casually, 'Who's the lucky fellow?'

It wasn't until he had nodded goodbye and she had heard the front door close that Emma even began to understand what he was talking about. 'Lucky fellow?' Did he think she had been practising with a boy friend? Could Colin Prentice take her even halfway along such a road?

Everything was a hopeless jumble, her nerves still jangled, so she wandered along to the kitchen and started preparing breakfast. Uncle Louis would be down in a minute. What could she tell him? That Nicholas Voss had called in on his way north? That he had plans for turning Whitewayes into a transit camp, and she, Emma, had no intention of letting him get away with it? Uncle Louis would agree. She plonked the kettle on the stove and began slicing bread. No need to tell Louis about all the other business. That was private, something to be sorted out between her and Nicholas. The phone rang and Emma sighed. Another hectic day had begun.

During the three following hectic days there wasn't much time to do anything except concentrate one hundred per cent on the job in hand. But it was the nights that presented Emma with most of her problems. The nights — and Nicholas.

And the nights started as soon as the last visitor had left the house, when the park was closed, and she and Louis were finally alone. Whether it was cooking supper, walking the gardener's dog or soaking in a bath, these were all leisure hours to be filled with the most important topic on her mind.

Uncle Louis had turned out his light ages ago. Emma's bath water had gone cold, so she juggled the hot tap and replenished it. The bathroom soon became steaming again, and she sank down once more; warm, comfortable — ready to drift into a blissful state of half-truths, half-beliefs, when all the confusion of her affair with Nicholas just didn't exist, and she could relive the time they had spent together last week, remembering only the exciting renewal of his physical attention.

The face that had stared down at her imperiously, with its dark brows arched in speculation, once more became the face of the man she loved. Loved with every nerve end — every positive thought. Long ago he had used those long lashes to tickle her cheek. Emma smiled, in spite of everything, and trailed a trickle of water from the sponge. But now those long lashes were being used as a veil — not of his thoughts, for he made those perfectly clear, but of the very man himself. What had happened to the Nicholas Voss she remembered? Had he lost his soul in some dark alley —

in some strange disillusion of the past?

And you're living in a fool's paradise, she told herself sharply, if you think the old days can return. They're gone, my girl, gone, do you hear? She sat up and began scrubbing herself briskly. From now on he's the enemy. You'll just have to get used to hating him.

It was very late when she finally climbed out of the bath. But it didn't matter – the house was closed on Mondays – and she would be able to have a lie-in tomorrow.

The intention was honourable, if not practical. The phone woke her just after eight the next morning. The park would be open as usual, and so would the cafeteria, but it appeared the gardener's wife had been taken ill, there would be no one to serve tea after the morning help left at two o'clock. Emma groaned. She had planned to have lunch in town. Colin wouldn't be very happy. She sighed and struggled out of bed, shivering in her thin nightie as she mentally readjusted her day. If she started now she could get everything done by lunch time, then she could spend the rest of the afternoon dispensing refreshments.

She was surprised to see Louis down to breakfast and he was equally surprised to see her.

'You're sure you don't mind helping out?' he asked, buttering a slice of toast with delicate, precise strokes.

'No one gets ill on purpose,' Emma shrugged. 'There's no alternative.'

'But it's your day off.' Louis sighed into his beard. 'If only we could afford more staff, have one or two people to fall back on ...'

'That's what I'm here for,' said Emma quickly. 'We've always managed in the past – we'll manage today.'

'Of course you will, my dear.' Louis was brisk once more. 'It's just that I'd arranged to go back to the flat. Start sorting out a few things – if I'm to be moving back in the next few weeks I'd like to get organised.'

Apart from packing his clothes, Emma couldn't see what there was for Louis to do – but there was no point in him staying on here; she couldn't exactly imagine him serving tea and buns to the locals.

'I suppose there's no chance of you closing the cafeteria this afternoon,' he suggested helpfully.

Emma shook her head. 'We've a nature ramble from the local primary school wandering round after lunch. The teacher said they'd like to come in around threeish. Someone's got to be there – we can't let them down.'

'I thought you were having lunch in town with young Prentice,' Louis continued, after taking a sip of coffee.

'I'll have to put him off,' Emma began. 'What's

the matter? Why are you pulling that face?'

'My dear, I never pull faces,' he chided softly. 'But this coffee – I don't believe you put in a pinch of salt.'

Emma hid a smile. Louis was the only person she knew who would have noticed.

'I really am getting quite worried about you these days,' he went on, drinking the deficient brew nevertheless. 'Your mind only seems half on your job. One might almost say you're acting like a woman in love.' Wily grey eyes twinkled mischievously before he picked up the *Daily Telegraph*. 'Good heavens!' he exclaimed, after rustling his way through a few pages. 'Young Woodford is marrying the Dunster girl.'

Emma leant across the table and peered over the top of the paper. 'Well,' she began firmly, 'you're not likely to see an announcement of my wedding to Colin.'

Uncle Louis turned a page before replying. 'I never suggested anything of the sort,' he said, with a touch of hurt pride.

Emma ruffled the top of his head as she began clearing the table. But it ought to be a very good idea. Colin Prentice was just the sort of man who would make an ideal husband. It was he who ought to be filling her first waking moments – and last sleeping thoughts at night.

And who but Colin would accept their cancelled

lunch so kindly, or spend the afternoon with her, helping behind a cafeteria counter?

'Word's getting round that Nicholas Voss is looking for an assistant,' he said, between a lull in customers. 'Any chance of you putting in a good word for me?'

Emma stared up at the tall blond figure in absolute astonishment. Had the world gone crazy? Was everyone conspiring against her? Surely it wasn't too much to expect Colin to be on her side?

'Why do you want to work for him?' she asked, trying to sound normal. 'What's wrong with the auctioneering business? I thought you were happy where you were.'

Colin shrugged, a lock of fine hair falling over his forehead. 'You know I'd like a place of my own one day,' he said quietly. 'Working in a Mayfair antique business would be a great experience, Emma.' He glanced down at her sideways and she fiddled with a row of empty cups. 'I'm looking ahead – thinking of the future ...' He trailed off and she didn't comment. They were back to the old, unspoken subject. He never went further, as if sensing that he would be rejected if he said more. But it was always there, hanging in the atmosphere between them. One day, thought Emma, yes – one day it would feel right. But not yet. No. She mentally shook herself. Surely someone as *worthy* as Colin was bound to capture her love.

'I don't think I have any influence with Nicholas Voss,' she said after a few moments, and she could tell it took Colin a few seconds to come back to the original subject. He smiled faintly and leant his elbows on the counter. He had a slow, relaxed manner. He soothed all before him. A big, beefy man, whom Emma teased would one day turn to fat if he wasn't very careful. 'You ought to take up Rugby,' she had said, time and time again; but he only shrugged and drifted into a sleepy contemplation of life, as he was now, appearing engrossed in the delicate icing on a cake. Most men would be nursing a hurt pride after another rejection. Emma felt guilty; maybe she was making a mistake. Maybe all you could ask for was a faithful, kind man who loved you. All the other business – she thought of Nicholas and felt a twist of pleasure dart through her – all *that* didn't have anything to do with the lasting love of marriage, did it? She served two more teas, Colin supplied the buns and took the money. It was a brief and thankful respite from bewildering thoughts.

The school party arrived, chairs were scraped back and turmoil reigned for several minutes until everyone's order had been taken and refreshments dispensed. But a calamity occurred as someone's hot chocolate was spilled over a table and it was Colin who sallied forth with a cloth to restore order out of chaos.

He was so good with children. Another advantage, Emma noted. But were good points enough? Shouldn't there be something else? But what? She sighed. Forget it, she thought. You have enough troubles to worry about at the moment without adding Colin to the list.

So instead of watching him, she let her eyes wander round the lofty converted coach-house, where sparrows hopped between tables searching for crumbs. They came in high up in the roof; something ought to be done about it. Emma sighed, but secretly she wanted the sparrows to stay, they were one of her first memories of Whitewayes when she had been brought here as a child. The idea of countless generations of small birds upholding the tradition was comforting, like the ravens at the Tower of London. Yes, as long as there were sparrows at Whitewayes the house would survive. Even Nicholas Voss couldn't control the instincts of wild life.

He couldn't control it – and neither were they perturbed when the door opened and a chilly, damp breeze ushered the arrival of the man uppermost in Emma's thoughts at that moment. The sparrows didn't seem to notice him, but Emma certainly did; and his unexpected arrival brought a touch of danger into the peaceful scene. She expected him to close the door behind him, but he didn't, someone else was following him. Emma tried not to appear intrigued, or even to have noticed their arrival. She fiddled with some chocolate rolls wrapped in silver paper. The other person was a woman, and Nicholas was escorting her; he took her arm and gently steered her towards the counter.

Emma looked up at last, marshalling every ounce of willpower to greet him calmly. She even managed a smile. For some unknown reason it seemed important to appear on good terms with him.

'What are you doing here?' Disapproval came from his stance, the stiffness of broad shoulders, the certain set of his head and the way he looked down at her with veiled, mysterious eyes. But the tone had been ambiguous, one might almost say concerned. But Emma wasn't fooled for one moment. And neither, it appeared, was his companion. Her delicate lips compressed to hide a smile. Emma tried not to look at her.

'We're a bit short-staffed,' she explained, as Colin watched the proceedings from the other side of the room. Perhaps he would come over and help.

'Do you usually have to do this kind of thing?' Nicholas was saying, glancing round with fatalistic gloom at the fading paintwork. 'Isn't Monday usually your day off?' he added suddenly, looking down at her with his bright penetrating eyes.

Emma felt exposed, as if he could read her mind;

so she looked uncertainly at the woman beside him to break the spell.

Nicholas took the hint and introduced them. 'This is Gail Weston,' he said simply, 'a client of mine. For some reason she seems very interested in Whitewayes.' He shrugged playfully. 'So I've brought her to look round.' And they smiled at each other, as if they were sharing some private joke.

A small hand clad in black leather gently touched his arm. 'Of course I'm interested, darling,' Gail Weston purred. 'If you're deserting us in town, someone has to see what the attraction is. And as I've already said – it's a very charming house.' Emma was dismissed with a flurry of long lashes.

Nicholas acknowledged her comment with a gracious inclination of his dark head. 'Wait till you see the inside,' he said seriously, taking her comment at face value. But Emma wasn't so simple. Gail Weston had wondered if there was female opposition at Whitewayes – and had obviously decided there wasn't.

'The first owner had it built for his mistress,' Nicholas was explaining, 'a charming lady – I must show you their correspondence some day. A very sad story by all accounts.'

While he talked, Emma watched them both; the tall, dark man so much at ease with life, so much in command of this and any situation; and the woman: Emma's first impression of fair, delicate beauty was enhanced now that she had the time to observe her. A neat, couturier suit, upswept hair without one strand out of place, and the sort of face that inspires men to climb mountains. How could anyone be put together so perfectly? Emma wondered. Not a crease, or splash of mud, and her voice was silvery — delicate, yet expressive. And as they talked, with Emma momentarily forgotten, there was an intimacy in their manner that said more than any words. Nicholas was in love with this woman — and she with him. It didn't take much intelligence to work that out. Emma reeled and clung on to the counter for support. Where was Colin? Why didn't he come over and get her out of this predicament?

'So we'll just go through,' said Nicholas, when he had explained some of Whitewayes' intrigues to Gail Weston. 'We tried to get in the house from the front,' he continued, 'but there was no reply. Is Louis out?'

'He's in town for the day,' Emma confirmed. 'He offered to stay,' she added quickly when she saw Nicholas' eyes narrow. 'But it was quite unnecessary. I'm perfectly able to cope.'

'No doubt.' His tone was measured. 'If you'll come this way, Gail.' He took her arm again. 'Through the kitchen, I believe,' he said, almost apologising, and Emma nodded, lifting a section of the counter for them to get through.

Gail Weston gathered herself together, making sure she didn't touch anything as she followed Nicholas. Their visitor showed absolutely no interest in these surroundings, and Emma realised there was no place in her world for the mundane necessities of life.

'Through there,' Emma indicated a door at the other end of the kitchen, 'then down the corridor – you'll see were it brings you out. You can't get lost,' she added, and Nicholas looked at her quickly. He had caught the sudden change in her voice – the hope that they definitely would get lost. Emma closed her eyes and prayed. She must be more careful – keep a guard on herself when he was about. How was it going to be possible? When would it stop hurting? Why did he have to make things worse by bringing along a girl friend?

'So we've been honoured by the royal presence,' said Colin, when Emma wandered back out behind the counter. The schoolchildren were beginning to shuffle out, one of the teachers was waving goodbye; the confusion gave her time to gather her wits. 'Gail Weston,' Colin explained, when she didn't comment. 'The grand lady herself. They say she keeps a pretty close eye on our Mr. Voss.' He pulled a face and winked. 'Mind you,' he confessed, 'can't say I'd mind if she felt like keeping a close eye on me. Perhaps that's what they mean by the luck of Old Nick.' He chuckled, and Emma found herself suddenly laughing. Oh, Colin was so good for her. He put everything into perspective. A week ago Nicholas Voss was only a hazy memory of the past. She would just have to learn to return him to the past. He didn't belong here and now. She would just have to try and pretend he didn't exist.

But it wasn't easy. Colin stayed until they closed the cafeteria at four o'clock, but then he had to go; no amount of entreating would make him stay and meet Nicholas. 'I'd like to work for him,' he said, as Emma helped him shrug into his coat. 'But perhaps it would be best if I approached him my-self,' he suggested, kissing her goodbye briefly, and his soft grey eyes didn't meet hers. It was almost, she thought afterwards, as if Colin sensed that knowing her wouldn't be a recommendation in Nicholas' eyes. But that was being silly. To feel like that, Colin would have to know about their past affair – and of course he didn't.

Emma sighed, and hung her large borrowed overall on the back of the kitchen door. Everything was tidy, ready for the morning. All Emma wanted to do now was to sit down and put up her feet.

The door marked 'Private' was slightly ajar. Had Uncle Louis returned? A smile was already on her lips as she walked into the sitting room. Nicholas Voss was well out of the way – she had checked from the side window – there hadn't been a car parked anywhere.

'Well timed,' said a deep voice from the fireside. 'Gail wouldn't stay, but I've made us some tea.' He peered round the back of a tall fireside chair. 'I hope you don't mind,' he added, as an afterthought. 'Can I pour you a cup?'

Emma nodded. She didn't trust herself to speak, much less perform a task that would show him how much her hands were shaking. She flicked an imaginary speck of dust from her sleeve and strolled across to the fire, sinking into a chair opposite his. While he busied himself at the trolley she tried not to stare at his back; at the way his dark jacket stretched smooth and wide, making her want to reach out and touch him. His hair was shorter than it used to be. Before, it had touched his collar, but now his neck was just visible in a tanned strip about the width of her finger. His hair was still thick and soft, she noticed, remembering the times her fingers had run through it, as she had drawn him closer, down to her, where so much strength and pent-up energy had been kept in tight control. Until that last time in the boat ...

'Your tea.' Emma blinked, flushed, and wondered if he was reading her mind again. He stood over her, holding out the cup, and finally she was obliged to take it. His lips were compressed in a tight line and he watched her take a hesitant sip.

'It's fine,' she mumbled, because he seemed to be expecting her to say something. But he wasn't bothered about the tea, she could tell. The room was suddenly alive with all the unspoken words in the gulf between them.

How many times had she imagined meeting him again? Taking tea with him, talking with him, sitting beside a fire on a winter's afternoon ... And it was really happening at last. He was here with her; Nicholas Voss. The man she loved — and always would love. You couldn't stop loving someone just because they had stopped loving you. Or had he ever really loved her? But what did it matter? Nothing would alter how she felt — nothing, ever.

He finally poured himself another cup and returned to his seat, moving a pile of papers on his table so that he could put down his cup. There was a box, a sort of jewel box, and he saw Emma looking at it with interest.

'I was showing Gail,' he said, picking up the box and pressing the catch with a strong thumb nail. The lid flew open and Emma gasped. Inside was a pendant, the simplest, most beautiful thing she had ever seen — a single emerald hung in a halo of delicate filigree gold. The chain was a perfect match. Resting on black velvet, it was a gift fit

for a queen. 'Don't you recognise it?' he asked,
looking across at her from behind his lashes. There
was an odd catch in his voice, but then there would
be. It was respect and a certain emotion for such
a magnificent work of art.

'It's the same pendant as the girl's in the portrait,' she said excitedly. 'The one at the top of the
stairs. How did you get it? Is it a copy?'

He shook his head. 'It's a family heirloom; it
belonged to one of my ancestors.'

'You mean *her*,' Emma gesticulated vaguely.
'The first owner of Whitewayes. She was a relation
of yours as well?'

'Is it so surprising that we share her? It was a
long time ago, Emma. Families spread – rather like
Queen Victoria and her tribe.'

'Why should you have the pendant?' said
Emma, when he had closed the lid and put the
box back in his briefcase. 'I mean,' she shrugged,
'shouldn't it belong to the estate or something?'
She hadn't meant to sound suspicious, but Nicholas
was quick to recognise the tone.

'Oh, it's mine, Emma, make no mistake,' he
said sharply. 'Ask Louis if you doubt me. The only
person entitled to wear it is the mistress of Whitewayes.' He paused. 'I suppose you could say I'm
keeping it, until such a time ...' He picked up the
delicate china cup and took a sip of tea. Strong,
well-manicured hands clasped the fragile piece

with all the tender care of an artist, but inside, Emma knew, he was quietly smouldering at her unguarded comment. She had dared to challenge him. Nicholas Voss wouldn't care for such treatment. What would he do?

'Louis phoned just before you came in,' said Nicholas, glancing up from his contemplation of the fire. 'He says he's been invited to dine out at Malden and you're not to worry if he doesn't make it home tonight.'

Emma nodded her thanks and shrugged. It was about time Louis enjoyed himself. He had spent far too many evenings here with only herself for company.

Nicholas slowly rose from the chair and strolled across to the tea trolley. 'He seemed rather worried at leaving you here on your own,' he continued, picking up a macaroon and breaking it in half. 'So I told him not to, that I would stay here. Gail was quite happy to take my car and drive herself home.'

'Stay here?' Emma was out of her chair in a flash. 'No, you can't – I mean there's no need, I assure you.'

'Isn't there?' A strange smile hovered round his mouth, a mixture of fatalism and determination. 'I think there's every need to stay, Emma.' He took the cup from her hand and put it gently on the trolley behind him. He was so cool, so self-assured, and all Emma could do was stare at him in horror. 'You see,' he continued, turning to face her once more, 'I'm still waiting for an answer to my question. Yes, *that* question,' he added, when she started. 'And although I'm a very patient man, Emma, five years is a very long time.' She held her breath while he stared at her. The clock ticked, the fire crackled — yet all else was silence as his face gradually underwent a tormenting change: anger, desperation, a final unleashing of every emotion he had kept in tight control. When he finally spoke it was with the dreadful knowledge that from now on there would be no going back to the safe neutrality of the past few days. Everything was about to explode, and Nicholas confirmed her theory by announcing forcefully, 'I've had enough, Emma. My patience has come to an end. I'm going to do what I should have done a long time ago!'

CHAPTER THREE

'And exactly what should you have done a long time ago?' Emma demanded, drawing herself upright and trying to appear calm.

'You mean you don't know?' Nicholas threw back his head and gave a brief contemptuous laugh from deep in his throat. 'You mean you still do it? It's an everyday occurrence?' the mock humour suddenly vanished, leaving his face cold, hard and impenetrable. 'In that case,' he went on, 'perhaps you won't mind telling me just how many men you've run away from – after they've asked you to marry them.'

The room spun round. This shouldn't happen to anyone *twice*, thought Emma frantically. It wasn't fair. Why was he tormenting her like this? His accusation hung in the air between them and she knew she had to say something quickly. The longer the delay the more she would acknowledge all the suffering and pain.

'Run away?' she repeated, at last. 'I – I suppose I did.' She shrugged, achieving the nonchalance she desperately strived for. 'It was reaction, I guess – I really can't remember.' She was hedging, playing for time, trying to think of some excuse that would satisfy this man.

She watched him now, standing with his back towards the fire in the position he was already adopting as his own. His tall, intimidating figure did more than block out the firelight – it made her feel cold and frightened inside. There was no warmth in the high cheeks, in the stiff, unbearing way he watched her minutely. He looked like a man waiting for a sentence to be passed, as if he expected her to explain her rejection of him ... And then Emma suddenly realised. That was to be her escape. Nicholas Voss wasn't used to women turning him down. If she attacked his pride, maybe he wouldn't notice the hollowness of her words.

'You must have thought me a strange little thing,' she began uncertainly, returning to her chair with an assumed air of confidence. 'Of course, I shouldn't do it now – if the same thing happened again,' she explained, and somehow the words came out steadily enough. 'I mean, at my age,' she continued, glancing up and meeting his unwavering eyes. '*Now*, I would be able to find the words – to explain ...' She trailed to silence, that was quite enough to say at one go.

'Explain!' The word shot out, obviously louder than Nicholas had intended. 'But that's precisely what I've been waiting for, Emma,' he continued, this time in a cool, controlled voice. 'That's what

I've been waiting for for five years.'

'It's – nothing so very special, really.' Her voice sounded shrill, she steadied it. 'A lovely summer was one thing, but marriage – well, quite honestly, Nicholas,' she paused, having to scrape every ounce of willpower to pronounce her condemnation, 'it just wouldn't have worked, you see. There was – *is*,' she corrected hastily, 'too much of a difference between us.'

'You mean in age?' he interrupted, and Emma was grateful for a chance to gather her wits. She had actually said it. The truth finally admitted at last. Later – in her bed and alone – then she would cry all the tears that were welling up inside.

'A difference in age?' She made it sound only a slight problem. 'I suppose there was that. I was only eighteen and you were – well,' she shrugged again, 'it was quite a difference, anyway.'

'Ten, eleven years, did it seem a lot to you, Emma? Does it still seem a lot?' he added. The sides of his cheeks were drawn inwards, shadows played in the dark hollows.

Emma pretended to think, to weigh judgements, and Nicholas seemed content to allow her a respite. But all her judgements had been made years ago. Ten years, no, what difference could age make? But it was the living, the experience, during those years that counted. Couldn't he see that? And as she had grown older so had he. There would be no catching up – ever. The chasm was as wide, as unscaleable as before. She would never have the experience of life to match his. How, in those circumstances, could she ever hope to keep the attention of his love? Even then she had known all this instinctively, but she had run away instead of facing it. But it had to be faced – here, now. At least it would put an end to any glimmer of hope she might secretly have cherished all these years.

She looked up at Nicholas and found him still watching her. Firelight danced behind him, his silhouette was tall, dark, intimidating. She had to say something – and make it sound totally convincing.

'I suppose I just didn't love you – it was as simple as that,' she said, directing her gaze down to his black shoes planted firmly on the fireside rug. She waited for the outburst, the fiery tirade to fall on her head – but nothing happened.

At last Nicholas exhaled slowly, wearily, as if the weight of years had been suddenly lifted. Emma was instantly alert to his new mood. He wasn't in the least bothered that she hadn't loved him, in fact, he seemed almost relieved.

'So it wasn't because I – frightened you?' he asked surprisingly.

Frightened? Emma stared back at him. Did he mean frightened of being seduced? If it hadn't been sad it would have been almost funny. Yes, she had been frightened, but not of his love. No, frightened of the experienced complexities of his life. It set him so much apart – and cast herself into a void of despair. But she mustn't sink into it – mustn't let Nicholas see how desperately she was fighting for survival.

'Frighten me?' This time she said the words out loud. Laughing, scornful. 'Not in the way you think – not for what you might have done . . .' She trailed off, letting his imagination do the rest.

'You didn't mind having a good time – you were just frightened because I asked you to marry me?' He didn't expect an answer; but now that the matter was finally cleared up it seemed to give him no peace. Instead he appeared to withdraw even more into himself, as he had on his first visit to Whitewayes early on Thursday morning. 'I see.' He nodded down to his chest, the top of his dark head visible for several moments as he remained in contemplation of the floor. 'Then there really is no need to discuss the matter further,' he said eventually, raising his eyes to look into her strained face. 'What a waste,' he almost whispered, looking blindly past her; almost, she thought, as if he was looking down the endless corridor of time. Five years of time. But why had he thought them a waste?

'Of course, it would have made things a lot easier if you had said all this before.' Now author-

ity was back in command, his shoulders were
businesslike – his stance once more that of the
new controller of Whitewayes.

Emma bristled. 'I think I made my feelings perfectly clear,' she managed to say with great diffi-
culty. 'It's hardly my fault if you've been under
the wrong impression all this time.'

He nodded again, only now his head was held
back so that he was staring down his nose at her.
Mobile, dark eyebrows raised fractionally, the
mouth curved to a cynical smile.

'Naturally it's not your fault, my dear Emma,'
he almost purred, but it was the cautious murmuring of a wildcat; deep, husky and threatening. 'The
mistake has been all mine for even supposing that
you had such delicate, sensitive feelings.' She was
about to retort, but his look stopped her. 'But now
we can put all that behind us,' he continued, walking over to his briefcase which he had left beside
the settee. 'Now we can return to the real reason
for my visit – the important matter in hand. I want
to tell you exactly what I have in mind for Whitewayes,' and his voice and look were that of a
total stranger.

His plan was clear, concise. Lecturers had already been approached, the first weekend course
arranged for mid-March, the publicity was to
begin immediately.

'There'll be no need to give precise details at

this stage,' he said, leaning back in the chair and crossing his long legs. 'We can arrange the syllabus nearer the time, but I want to discuss the accommodation with you – decide exactly how many guests we can take. There might have to be extensive alterations.'

Emma closed her eyes in horror. This was exactly what her father had feared most.

'Alterations? You can't – I mean,' she stumbled, 'you can't knock down walls. It isn't allowed – there's a preservation act or something.'

'Of which I'm very well aware,' he sighed. 'Really, Emma ...' Irritation was creeping into his voice; he paused, breathing deeply, before continuing. 'But obviously several of the small rooms will have to be converted into bathrooms – showers. Rooms will have to be reorganised – *changes* made,' he added forcefully. 'Extra staff ... The list is endless.'

'I don't doubt it!' Angry topaz eyes flashed across at him. One thing could be said in Nicholas Voss' favour – he certainly made it easy to hate him. It was all just as terrible as her father had predicted. Whitewayes would become an institution – bare-boarded and functional. Surely there must be some way she could stop him.

But although no immediate idea presented itself to Emma, it seemed that Nicholas wasn't suffering from the same problem. He had countless ideas.

Too many of them, she realised, if he was only
supposed to have known of this appointment since
last week.

'The first course – in March,' he was saying now,
'will be about art appreciation. We certainly have
enough paintings at Whitewayes to more than
cover a weekend syllabus. Then, later on, I thought
we'd cover furniture, and maybe porcelain –
silver.' He sifted through a bulging briefcase and
handed across a slim pamphlet. 'This is the type
of thing I thought we'd send round to the local
libraries,' he explained, handing Emma what she
judged to be a printer's proof. There was a line
drawing of the house with its name beneath – a
rather attractive piece of work, she had to admit –
giving brief details of the pleasures to come. All
this couldn't possibly have been organised in just
a few days. Nicholas Voss had known he was coming to Whitewayes for some considerable time.
Yet he had wanted to keep it a secret. Why? So
that he could present Emma with a *fait accompli*?
But he might find that difficult to accomplish without the co-operation of his assistant. And that was
one thing Nicholas certainly hadn't achieved.

Not only did she then have to show him all over
the house; the spare rooms upstairs kept for reno-
vating and storing special items; the lofty ballroom, drawing room and library downstairs, as
well as all the kitchens and sculleries – but she also

had to cook the wretched man's supper!

'There really is no need for you to stay,' she had tried again, when they had finally finished their reconnoitre and had returned to the sitting room to switch on lamps and draw the curtains. But Nicholas had been adamant. He had promised Louis.

Emma bit the insides of her cheeks and marched from sink to stove and back again. And that was another thing, she decided, banging pots and pans and splashing water all over the window. Before very long she was going to have a serious talk with dear Uncle Louis. She had an idea he was more involved in all this that he would care to admit.

'Supper will be ready in five minutes – I'm just going to dish up,' she finally announced to the back of his chair, before disappearing again and trudging along to the kitchen. The phone was ringing by the time she returned, but luckily there was an extension hanging on the wall.

'Hullo, it's me!' For some reason it took Emma several seconds to recognise Colin's voice. He was being gentle, apologetic – trying to say sorry for appearing a bit 'off' when they had parted.

'Really, I hadn't given it another thought,' said Emma, trying to make it sound like a white lie, when in fact it was nothing but the truth. Had he been 'off'? She tried to remember. Oh, yes, in the cafeteria. 'It's sweet of you to phone,' she said at last, 'there was really no need – but thanks.'

She sensed he felt relieved at having done the right thing. 'I had a lot on my mind, I guess,' he admitted, sounding as if he was all set for a long chat. Emma glanced at the potatoes bubbling away on the stove and hoped they wouldn't turn to pulp. 'Thinking about getting a new job, and every-thing,' he was saying now, and Emma tried desper-ately to concentrate. 'I thought I'd phone Nicholas Voss first thing in the morning – arrange an inter-view,' Colin continued. 'No point in dithering – I can't let the grass grow under my feet.'

Emma was on the point of saying he could talk to Nicholas now, but something stopped her. 'Good idea,' she said instead.

'I'll let you know what happens.'

'Yes – do.' She was desperately trying to sound interested, to think of something else to say, but there were footsteps coming down the hall. They were getting closer. 'Look – I'm sorry,' she stumbled into the receiver, 'but I really must go – supper's nearly boiling over.' Their goodbyes were brief, she could tell Colin was puzzled, but at least she had the phone back on its hook before Nicholas came into the room.

His eyes met hers briefly, as if he was expecting her to say something, to comment on the phone call, but of course she didn't, and his mouth formed itself into a thin smile.

'I hope I didn't interrupt anything,' he said, obviously quite delighted that he had.

'Just a friend,' Emma shrugged, straining the potatoes and reaching for the butter and milk. Nicholas stood watching as she began beating them together. He was thinking, pondering over the situation, she could almost hear his brain ticking over.

Emma moved with short, jerky movements, feeling guilty about not mentioning Colin. But why? It was quite ridiculous, yet she was sure Nicholas was aware of her mood and the atmosphere intrigued him.

Eyes as blue as the bright summer sky regarded her down the length of the dining table, when supper was eventually served.

'You really shouldn't have gone to all this bother,' he exclaimed, glancing around the elegant room, before helping himself to more vegetables. 'An omelette in the kitchen would have been perfectly adequate.'

Emma had guessed as much – Nicholas had never been any problem over food. But a cosy meal in the kitchen would have been altogether the wrong approach. Here, with six feet of shining mahogany between them, it was possible to retain her composure. The chandelier sparkled above their heads, silver and crystal gleamed on the sideboard. It wasn't really a large room, but the cream carpet and light walls contrasted graciously with the dark antique furniture. Although it was a bit chilly. Maybe the kitchen would have been better after all.

'How many people do you think this room would take?' asked Nicholas, after another speculative sweep of his blue eyes.

'Eight, comfortably,' said Emma, misunderstanding. 'But there's a separate extension leaf that can be fitted in, so I suppose it could take twelve. I think we had that many a couple of Christmases ago.' She stopped, her fork hovering in mid-air. He didn't mean around the table, she realised at last. He meant how many people could the room accommodate. How many guests? Come to that – how many *tables*?

They stared at each other as comprehension dawned.

'Surely you don't intend using this as the dining room?' she said at last.

'And why not?' he challenged. 'It's fairly near the kitchen. I think our guests would prefer to have their food served reasonably hot.'

Guests! They weren't guests. Invaders, more like. And this wretched man was leading the troops. This was where she had to be particularly clever.

'You'd need a lot of little tables, where would this one go?' she began, trying to sound reasonable. 'And you can hardly serve twenty-odd people from *that* sideboard. No!' She shook her head quite determinedly. 'You need something larger – more functional. The small amount of staff we're going to be able to afford won't have time to take care of the furniture. We'll have to prepare one of the empty rooms in the other wing – get hot plates, or specialise in a cold table,' she added with a little laugh. Even humouring him was better than allowing the masses in here. Her father – and Uncle Louis – would have a fit.

'You're right, of course.' Nicholas dabbed his mouth with a napkin, then gazed at her over the rim of his glass. 'You always had such good sense, my dear Emma,' he purred, yet the soft timbre of his voice carried easily down the long table. 'I knew it was only a matter of time before you saw things my way. Naturally we shall use one of the other rooms. Which do you suggest?'

Too late, Emma saw that she had been manoeuvred into a corner. She had forgotten Nicholas' skill at manipulation, so she seethed quietly and just shrugged. Luckily he didn't insist on an answer, but there was a faint gleam in his eye. And the fine edge of tension was there between them as strong as ever.

The silence grew – thickened – save for the gentle scraping of knives and forks. Occasionally Emma glanced at him through her lashes. Dark, enigmatic features masked every emotion from his face, yet was he really feeling as calm as he looked? Nonchalantly sipping his wine, deftly removing chicken from a bone, all with the casual self-assurance of an experienced man of the world.

Emma's cheeks grew stiff with tension, her palms felt moist, the food had to be chased around her mouth for ages before she could even hope to swallow it. So he finished first, and now she had to struggle on, while brilliant eyes coolly surveyed her.

The evening dragged on in the same way. By ten-thirty Emma knew there wasn't any chance of Uncle Louis arriving home tonight. Someone had to suggest bed – it wasn't going to be easy.

She turned another page of her book and looked across at Nicholas as he sat in Uncle Louis' chair. If only ... she thought wistfully, gazing at the shell of the man she had once loved. How handsome he was! The years had added to his attractiveness. Long, strong limbs relaxed in a deep chair, his tie and jacket discarded and replaced by a pale blue sweater that did wonderful things for his eyes. She noticed his brows still welded together as he frowned over something he was reading. A hand came up and he slowly and thoughtfully stroked his chin. What peace there seemed to be in the man. How she would have loved to ask what was bothering him – helped in some way. She sighed softly, turning another page without having read one word of it. But it was all an illusion – a fanciful dream. Things like that didn't happen in the real world.

'Would you like a hot drink before you go to bed?' she asked suddenly. There seemed to be something decidedly safe in offering a man a cup of cocoa.

He didn't want it, but he took the hint, gathering together bits and pieces and returning everything to his briefcase.

'The spare bed is made up,' Emma began awkwardly, when they were halfway up the curved staircase. 'But you'll need a towel, I'll – I'll just fetch one for you.'

He was right behind her as she opened the big airing cupboard doors and stood on tiptoe, trying to find a large white bath towel that didn't need mending. She pulled out everything but the right one, cursing softly as the pile began to slide. Any moment, she thought, and they would both be buried in towels.

Nicholas thought so too. She heard him laugh, then he came closer, easily reaching up and steadying the pile, but now his body was against her own, she heard his breath falter as it tangled with her hair – and suddenly it was raining towels all round them – she was being scooped into his arms. And then he began kissing her.

CHAPTER FOUR

EMMA thought she must be melting, dissolving, disappearing into him. There was nothing between them; in body or spirit. It was as if they were one being – one soul – one heart beating life's message through both their veins.

Everything was so real – so *exactly* right. Joy leapt and danced within her. It felt as if she had come home after a long, cold journey. Nicholas was breathing warmth and throbbing vitality deep within her.

For a while there was no urgency in his slow sensuous kisses. He was folding her closer against him; protective, enveloping, Emma was enmeshed in a tangle of sheer delight. She felt his breath in her hair ... against her ear, and then she realised he was whispering her name. Over and over ... 'Emma ...' This time tortuously, and when his lips sought hers again he was demanding, possessive of every inch of her face and the slender column of her neck.

'Emma,' he purred again. It was a low, husky sound, questioning, persuading, and she knew exactly what he was asking for. She wanted to say 'no', to push him away, but nothing happened except a reckless joy that threatened to overcome all else.

Why not – when it felt so right? When her need was as great as his. Now he was tugging at the ribbing of her sweater and a warm hand was coaxing its way between her shoulder blades. Her skin tingled; desire twisted and seared as sharp as any physical pain.

Time evaporated. Or was it her memory linking this occasion with that other occasion – in the boat – that summer so long ago? This was how it had been then. This wanting – this needing – this exciting, amazing man who could dominate with such skill. Could touch the very spot, the very spirit of Emma – the spirit that made her live.

And he could take her spirit soaring, upwards, on a plane of ecstasy. But it was towards a dangerous, unknown land, she had run away from that then ... Now something made her hesitate. Was she really afraid of that unknown place? Or was she afraid of Nicholas? Afraid of his ability at manoeuvring. Afraid that if she allowed this to happen she might come to depend on him. And what would happen when the time came for everything to end? What hope could there be in the emptiness of a world that had once held Nicholas Voss?

Questions ... doubts ... a crazy spinning in an

unsure tide of longing and dreams. Emma was gasping, trying to cry out. It was just all too much. She couldn't cope, couldn't bear to let him see how vulnerable she had become.

But he wasn't stopping, hadn't noticed her useless struggles. He thought she was playing, flirting. Strong arms knitted around her. Before, she had stayed through acquiescence – now she stayed through pure brute force.

'Nicholas ... please ... No, it won't work.' Somehow she gasped out her halting sentence. Only she wasn't getting through to him. He seemed desperately set towards his own goal. His face was tortuous, his hands and body sinuously intruding. One moment he seemed to be swept along with emotion ... and the next he was staring down at her, the blue of his eyes radiating disbelief.

'Nicholas ... there's no point.' This time she was through to him and they stared at each other in silent horror. If only she could run away again. But it was impossible. This time she had to stay and face him. 'I can't,' she said simply, seeing agony mirrored in his eyes.

'You want me as much as I want you.' The words hissed between narrow lips. He sounded quite unlike the Nicholas Voss she thought she knew. The hands on her arms remained fiercely tight – as if he was willing some strength of his own to be poured into her.

'But wanting isn't enough,' she tried again, squirming and twisting away.

'What more must you have? I want you, Emma. Don't you understand?' His expression became fierce; for a moment he looked exactly like one of the paintings down in the gallery. A wild chevalier – dark – satanic ... 'Emma!' This time he shook her. 'Tell me, what more do you want? What else do I have to say?'

'That you love me,' she wanted to cry out to him. 'That I won't be your funny little girl whose childish ways will soon tire you. That you won't mind me wearing jeans and tee-shirts and not bothering with make-up except for occasions. Tell me you don't like beautiful, sophisticated women; that they're a decoration – nothing more!' Oh, how easily the words came into her mind. If only ... if only she had the courage to breathe life into them.

But nothing came, as she knew it wouldn't. She beat frantically against his chest, tears misted her eyes and suddenly the bands of steel holding her had gone. She was free ... free to run along the landing and back down the gracious, curving staircase to the sanctity of the sitting room and the last dying embers of the fire.

Tears poured down her cheeks, but she didn't brush them away, and gradually they dried, leaving cold, tight streaks down her face.

The fire finally died, the room became chilly; for a while Emma didn't notice as she sat on the rug, her knees tucked under her chin, feeling as lonely and cold as the big, silent house seemed to be.

As the emotion within her tempered, she slowly became aware of the harsh external discomfort. She rubbed her arms, shivered, gazing around the darkened room, surprised, almost, to be there.

'You'd better get to bed, my girl,' she told herself sharply. 'Stop feeling sorry for yourself.' She struggled up, her knees were stiff, she had pins and needles in one foot, her comical hobble to the door managed to bring a faint smile to her lips.

But it didn't last long. Halfway up the stairs she saw the portrait again. The first mistress of Whitewayes, Nicholas had said. And there was the pendant, an emerald suspended in gold. How superb the original had looked lying on black velvet in its own special box!

Emma crept quietly along the landing, switching off lights as she went. All was silent. Nicholas seemed to be sleeping as quietly as the house, so she tiptoed into her own room, undressed in the darkness and slipped into bed.

What relief! Her body relaxed, but her mind

couldn't rest and soon she was lying on her back and staring at the ceiling. She kept seeing the portrait – and Nicholas – and then she remembered he had been showing the pendant to Gail. Why? Emma tossed and turned again. Maybe he had explained about the first owner not being married. Maybe he just happened to have the pendant on him ... and Gail had been interested ... It all seemed a bit far-fetched, a bit too well organised. In the same way that his overnight case had been a surprise. How convenient – almost as if he had known he would be staying the night.

'The sale in Derbyshire,' he had reminded her, when she had questioned the coincidence. 'Luckily I called in here on my way back – so I had everything with me.'

Emma had still been suspicious. Something remained to puzzle her. And now, in the black cosiness of her bed, sleep gradually seemed to be creeping up on her. Whitewayes ... the painting ... a pendant ... Nicholas and Gail. Round and round the images slowly drifted. Nicholas and Gail driving home from Derbyshire. Then Emma was wide awake, her heart hammering. They had been spending the weekend *together*! It was all the proof she needed. And he had been showing *her* the pendant ...

When the alarm bell finally rang it felt as if

she hadn't slept one wink. Emma dragged her weary body from the warm bed. Another day, another set of problems to overcome. But above all, the problem of Nicholas. For a second she paused, arms only half in her dressing-gown, eyes staring sightlessly towards the grey dawn behind the curtains. Had Nicholas really kissed her that way last night? Had they momentarily drawn close to each other? The memory returned, as if she was living it all again, the excitement and desire that for a moment had known no bounds. She closed her eyes and breathed deeply. What a treasure of living he had offered her! What a tantalising glimpse of his magical world of senses ... A noise outside in the park made her eyes fly open. She saw the dim, familiar room, the pink carpet, the crumpled bed from which she had risen on countless mornings before today. At last she struggled into the gown, fished for her slippers and tried to smile. Maybe Nicholas wasn't along the landing in the spare room. Maybe he was a million miles away from Whitewayes. Maybe last night had just been a dream ...

'A nightmare? What do you mean – a nightmare?' Uncle Louis repeated, smiling complacently across the lunch table.

'I've just been *telling* you,' Emma exclaimed, running impatient fingers through her short dark hair. Louis sighed disapprovingly, but she pretended not to notice. This time he wasn't going to put her off. 'Not only does Mr. Nicholas Voss install himself for the night,' she explained once more, 'but I've spent all the morning traipsing after him with a note pad while *he* decided which rooms will be used for the courses, which furniture is to be moved ... *He's* chosen the firm to do alterations upstairs. In fact, *everything*, Uncle Louis. He's thought of it all, obviously planned everything well in advance.' She paused, staring at her uncle shrewdly, and when he made no comment, she added. 'How long has he known he would be coming here? It couldn't have been since just last week. Is there any chance, d'you think, that someone may have had a quiet word in his ear?' It was a well known fact that Louis and several of the Trustees belonged to the same club.

Several spoonfuls of soup passed Uncle Louis' lips before he chose to reply. But first he pressed his napkin lightly against his whiskers, took a sip of water, and ran a well-manicured finger across the heavy damask cloth.

'Obviously, in such cases as this,' he began at last, 'some approach would have to be made towards the – ah – prospective candidate.' His wily grey eyes met hers, then flickered down to his soup. 'Especially in the circumstances,' he concluded, picking up his spoon again, but Emma wasn't convinced.

'What circumstances?' she asked, although it was quite clear Uncle Louis didn't want her to press the matter.

He shrugged. 'As a single man he would have a few problems,' he explained presently. 'No wife, you see. This kind of appointment, my dear Emma, requires a certain, shall we say, standard. A certain social life is expected. The Trustees can be very old-fashioned, they have strong principles, and Nicholas will need a hostess, especially,' he carried on quickly, 'if the full potential of the house is to be used.'

Emma stared at the top of his head as her uncle once more tackled his soup. Hostess? Entertaining? Did Nicholas really have a problem in that direction? Did Uncle Louis *agree* that Whitewayes should be turned into an institution?

No, of course Uncle Louis wouldn't agree normally. It was just that wretched man's persuasiveness. She closed her eyes and momentarily recalled the exact extent of Nicholas Voss and his persuasion. Surely there was *something* she could do to stop him. And then, like an answer from heaven, the telephone rang.

'I've got it!' Colin's voice was raised excitedly as soon as the bleeps stopped. She could hear traffic roaring behind him. Why was he phoning from a callbox? Got it? Got what? Emma stared stupidly at the receiver and blinked. 'He was out all the morning,' Colin went on, 'but his secretary said come along lunch time. So I did – I've been with him this past hour. I start at the beginning of next month.'

'Oh, that's great,' Emma enthused, more with relief that she had finally realised what he was talking about. 'I'm very pleased for you,' she added. And she was. If Colin wanted to work for Nicholas then that was his affair. Although she had a peculiar feeling that somehow it was going to complicate things.

'So how about celebrating?' he began.

'What?' But he had broken off in a panic at the sound of rapid bleeps.

'Haven't got any more change. I'll phone this evening from home. 'Bye, love ...' and there was only just time to say goodbye herself, although she wasn't sure if he heard her.

Unfortunately the celebrating had to wait a few days, until the following Sunday, in fact, when Colin came to lunch. It obviously wasn't the kind of treat he had intended, so to make up for it Emma left Uncle Louis in charge for a while and suggested she and Colin take a walk around the park.

'It seems ages since I've seen you,' he said, accepting the best of the situation. They were strolling through the copse now, and he gently pulled Emma's arm through his own.

How big and comfortable he was, she thought, as their bodies brushed together, keeping time with their footsteps. The weather had turned cold; the sky through the bare trees was a pale, wintry blue; the sinking sun, a streaky shade of yellow, stretched wide across the heath. It was the kind of day for a brisk pace, a cold nose, and crumpets by the fire at tea-time.

She looked up at Colin's massive bulk. 'You should have been a farmer,' she said with a laugh. 'You certainly don't look a dealer in fine arts ...' The laughter faded. Why did she have to say that? Why remind herself of Nicholas Voss? She had tried all week to forget him.

'Do you wish I was a farmer?' Colin asked, glancing down at her uncertainly.

She smiled and shrugged. How could you tell someone it didn't matter what they did? It didn't matter because it wasn't important. But it should have been. Emma frowned, cross with herself for not being more responsive.

It didn't take long to get through the wood and soon they were wandering along the path that skirted the trees. They could see the house again, the lawns rising majestically to meet the smooth white stone, mellowed now, in the late afternoon sun.

'Do you want to go back yet?'

Emma shook her head. 'Let's go down to the lodge,' she suggested, snuggling into his arm in an attempt to comfort. He looked pleased. 'They've had some puppies — about a fortnight ago,' she went on. 'I haven't liked to disturb them so far, but I should think it would be safe enough now.'

Their visit didn't create any problems for the proud mother. Lying on her side, the black and white spaniel displayed for all to see a fat stomach and a clutch of wriggling, smooth offspring.

'They're adorable,' Emma crooned, keeping her voice low and gentle as she knelt beside the box. That smelled warm, that odd mixture that made up a puppy smell; warm bodies, she supposed, and milk.

'Which one would you like?' asked Colin, when, having refused offers of tea, they were slowly wending their way back home.

'You mean a puppy?' Emma had been lost for a moment in her own private thoughts. 'Oh, no, I couldn't. Not in the house ... I'm sure it wouldn't be possible.'

They walked on in silence, their feet crunching on the gravel as they twisted their way down the narrow path. A couple of cars passed them, visitors leaving, it was probably nearly time to close the house. When it was safe to do so they walked side by side again, arms linked, looking like the two long standing friends that they were.

'Why don't you like Nicholas Voss?' asked Colin quite mildly, and Emma realised he hadn't been pondering the question of the puppy all this time.

'I don't,' she defended quickly. 'I mean, I don't *not* like him.' They both laughed, but Colin's face was soon serious again.

'You don't mind me working for him, then?' he continued in his determined way. 'I thought perhaps that you might,' he went on. 'I thought there was something,' he shrugged, 'but I'm not sure what ...'

'Silly old thing!' She shook his arm gently as they crossed the car park and made their way round to the side door. She could feel Colin watching her. He was always so frank and open, but for the first time she was aware of thoughts he wasn't sharing with her. She felt on edge, vulnerable, and for some reason gave a nervous little laugh. 'I haven't seen Nicholas for years,' she tried to assure him. 'We're practically strangers ...' How sad, but true, she thought suddenly. 'You probably know far more about him than I do,' she went on, as they finally went indoors and took off their coats. 'You must see him in town – at sales and things. In fact,' she went on, making her eyes flash and trying to sound as if she wanted a good gossip. 'In fact, you can probably tell me all about Gail Weston. You remember,' she coaxed, 'she came here with him the other day — when you were helping me in the cafeteria.'

For some reason Colin looked suddenly pleased — comforted, almost. How strange.

'You mean you don't know about the illustrious — *wealthy* — Mrs. Weston?' he remarked casually, crossing the hall with Emma and nodding 'good night' to the uniformed warden who was just beginning to lock up.

The sitting room was empty and they both stood before the fire, warming cold hands and faces, and Emma had to wait. Wait for Colin to sift through his memory and select just the right information. There was nothing to do but be patient. The fact that he took so long deciding exactly what he should tell her was no particular comfort.

'I don't know quite what you'd call it,' he began eventually. 'There's plenty of talk — there would be — but to be fair, I don't really know what they are to each other.'

That was carrying discretion too far. Emma could have screamed. 'Well, just tell me what people are saying,' she said quickly, and then stared back at the fire when Colin looked surprised.

'Just that she's got plenty of money. That they've been seeing each other regularly for four years now.'

'They were in Derbyshire together, last week-end,' Emma said, softly this time, and Colin nodded.

'Doesn't take much working out, does it?' he added. 'He isn't seen around with anyone else, and a man like Nicholas would need ...' He broke off uncertainly, but it was unnecessary for him to say more. Emma knew exactly what Nicholas Voss would need.

She easily pictured Gail Weston again. Of course she was Nicholas' type. He would want the woman standing beside him to have a certain presence. A certain self-assurance – a particular charm. Yes, that was the word. How many times had she heard Louis say of someone, 'she's such a *charming* woman'. That's what men really wanted. And the charming women were always mature, self-confident, and they didn't go around in faded sweaters and splashed jeans, nor play with puppies. Why did Emma ever allow herself to believe that she could make Nicholas happy?

'Is she married?' Emma asked after a while, in a voice so casual that it would have fooled her uncle if he had been there.

Colin shook his head. 'Her husband died five or six years ago, I believe. I guess she's what you'd call a very merry widow!'

CHAPTER FIVE

'You can't,' declared Emma. 'You simply can't move it. It's impossible, out of the question.' After two weeks of tapping and banging – builders everywhere – with no time to think, let alone get on with her work, now she had this wretched man wanting to move the Cézanne. A workman, in overalls and cap, thinking *he* could touch the masterpiece! It was just the final straw.

'It's the pipes, miss,' he tried to explain again.

'*Pipes!*'

'What exactly seems to be the trouble?' said another voice from the doorway.

Emma's face set in anger. She might have known he'd turn up now. That was all she needed!

'Ah, Mr. Voss.' The foreman, if no one else, looked relieved to see him. 'I've just been saying to Miss Price here, it's the pipes, you see, for the new water tank – there could be a bit of a leak and I thought . . .'

Emma suddenly saw what he had been getting at. Why couldn't he have said the same to her?'

'And the problem is?' Nicholas continued, coming into the ballroom now, his footsteps over the shining parquet sounding precise, staccato, like disapproving punctuation marks.

'Well,' the man hesitated, 'it's just in case there's an accident, Mr. Voss. You know, a bit of a leak, I thought it might be a good idea to take down this painting.' He jerked his thumb over his shoulder to indicate the one in question.

'That seems to be a very sensible precaution,' said Nicholas, his blue eyes wide, his voice matter-of-fact.

'But ...' Emma tried again.

'I think if you give us twenty minutes or so,' he went on, with one of his charming smiles, 'then Miss Price and I will see what we can do.'

The man nodded, thanked him, and made for the door. Emma, furious, beyond anything she had felt for days, started to follow him. 'Coming in here as if he owned the place,' she muttered. 'Interfering, making me look a right fool ...' But she didn't get any further. A cool voice from the centre of the ballroom called her back. Here we go, she thought quickly, turning round to face him, expecting the storm to break.

But it didn't. Nicholas' face was a mask of discretion. 'I just wanted to remind you about the lecturers' meeting. They'll be here shortly. Tea for five, if you please.' It was the cool order of a stranger. Emma nodded and left.

'Lecturers' meeting – tea for five. And I sup-

pose I have to change as well, wretched man.'
For a moment she was tempted to stay in her
jeans, but to make such a protest would be
demonstrating her anger and she didn't want to
appear as vulnerable as all that. Consequently,
when the tea trolley was eventually pushed into
the cosy sitting room, the girl behind it was suit-
ably clad in an oatmeal sweater-dress and casual
silk scarf tied around her neck. Uncle Louis
would frown, she knew. 'Most inelegant, you'll
be wearing a string of pearls and carrying lavender-
perfumed hankies next ...' But Colin said the
dress clung in all the right places, and Emma
smiled at the memory as she negotiated the
trolley around an awkward corner. Actually this
meeting might turn out to be better than she had
anticipated. At least it would make a pleasant
change to see a few new faces.

Only there weren't as many as she had
imagined. One swift glance around the room
revealed the usual inhabitants of Whitewayes
and only one stranger; a little man, going a bit
thin on top – and Colin. *Colin!* Emma stared
unbelievingly. Now all the intrigue – all those
words unspoken, suddenly rushed to meet her.
She should have told Nicholas about Colin. She
should have explained Nicholas *to* Colin. But it
was too late; she tried frantically to send him a
silent message, but of course he didn't understand

and in his usual good-natured way was rising to help her with the trolley.

'Hullo, love,' was Colin's simple greeting as he kissed her on the top of her head. 'This cake looks good; one of yours?'

Emma nodded and muttered something appropriate. She could feel her face stiffening as she willed the blush to go away. Nicholas remained seated, relaxing, with his long legs crossed, the fingers of one hand gently drumming a tattoo on the arm of his chair. She didn't dare to glance at him, but she didn't have to. The old electricity was back – she could feel it crackle in the air between them. Surely everybody must be conscious of the atmosphere.

She passed round cups and a steady conversation resumed, a little awkward, maybe, and halting. Everyone talked – except Uncle Louis. He just sat in his corner taking it all in. His old grey eyes twinkled mischievously. The rogue! Emma gave him one of her severe looks. He was actually enjoying all this!

'We've decided on groups of twenty,' Nicholas began, when the tea and chatting was over. 'We may expand later in the year, but to begin with – as far as space, organisation and catering goes – twenty will be enough to manage.'

Emma glanced casually around the little group. She had discovered they were all specialists in their field – Colin with his furniture, Louis silver, Nicholas painting and jewellery; and the little man was one of the Trustees, sent along to give official approval. Emma vaguely recognised him. They must have met some time over the past few years. It was just as well there was someone else here to stop Nicholas running riot, but the man seemed more intrigued with Emma than most other things. He asked how she had managed after her father's death and if she had enjoyed running Whitewayes for her brief term of office. They were altogether curious questions, she thought, wishing he would pay more attention to what was being said. She glanced at Nicholas across the low coffee-table festooned with paper-work. He was showing them all the advertising pamphlets, suggesting a timetable ...

'I trust you're making a note of all this,' he said quite sharply; his impersonal gaze hurting more than any harsh words.

'Of course.' Emma scribbled something on her pad, trying to remember what on earth he had said. But then her pen stopped and she was just watching him again as he talked concisely, his voice steady, persuasive, yet carrying with it absolute authority. '*We* have decided,' he had said. But they were really all *his* ideas. And did he really believe anyone would disagree?

He was wearing his navy blue suit today, it

was crisp, darkly formal, the pale blue shirt starched, almost crackling. It appeared he had dressed to fit his mood. The hard, angular lines on his face matched, as well, she noticed, and there were little creases of tension at the corners of his mouth.

'How long are the people actually going to be here?' asked Colin, in his pleasant, cheery voice, and Emma shifted her gaze to him. She felt herself smile inside. He was such a comfort. So dependable. Then what was missing? He was so gentle – and loving. He would be an excellent father and husband – and he'd make a lovely uncle. Now the smile came outside, on to her face. That was the problem. She regarded Colin as a large, cuddly brother. He didn't excite her, not like Nicholas ... Now her eyes swept back to the man who had the power to drive her crazy. He could do it with a look – with less than a touch – just by breathing, by being there ... Emma felt her pulses quicken, the memory of old pleasures returned bright and vivid – they took her breath away – then they were gone, pushed back with regret but absolute determination. Nicholas Voss didn't love her, and never would – what was the use of remembering?

'I imagine everyone will arrive for supper on the Friday, and we'll carry on until Sunday tea,' Nicholas was explaining. His eyes flickered over

Colin in a curious manner, almost as if he knew
what Emma had been thinking. 'Naturally, neither
of you will be expected to be here all over each
weekend,' he went on, his glance encompassing
Louis this time. 'And I realise it won't be easy
organising each of us to fit in with the others.
But we have to make a start somewhere ...' He
shrugged, and everyone nodded their agreement.
'Then let's begin with the second weekend in
March, gentlemen,' he continued, and they all
made appropriate notes in their diaries.

Gentlemen! Huh! What about me? Emma
wanted to challenge. But it appeared Mr. Voss
didn't have any plans for the female member of
the team.

'I thought, after supper on the Friday evening,'
Nicholas was saying now, 'about nine o'clock –
we'll have a short welcoming talk, about half
an hour or so. Simple stuff.' He pursed his lips.
'Explain who we are – tell them about Whitewayes, and give a general rundown of the sub-
jects we shall be covering for the time they're
with us. We'll have to organise a bar of some sort
– and I do want the lecturers to be available for
half an hour afterwards to make themselves
known and to help everyone settle in.

'Now, about these lectures.' He sat back in his
chair and interlaced long fingers into an arch,
upon which he rested his chin and peered at them

all thoughtfully. All of them, except Emma. He had stopped looking at her entirely, as if he chose to forget her existence. 'I want to get away from the formal "speaker" system ...'

I, I, I – want, want, want! Emma fumed inside but kept silent, as he went on.

'Colin knows what I mean. Mr. Prentice has just started running my Mayfair shop,' he added to the little Trustee man. 'We've both discussed it all at great length. Luckily, Colin is as enthusiastic about the whole scheme as I am.' Nicholas broke off, as if an idea had suddenly occurred to him. Emma saw the skin over his knuckles turn white, the lines around his mouth grow tighter, and one swift, penetrating glance from cobalt eyes sent her stomach twisting in fear. What was wrong? What had been said? But then the expression vanished, almost as if she had imagined it. His shoulders relaxed again; he gave a stiff smile.

'Where was I?' He said impatiently. 'Oh yes, the timetable. Well – lectures morning, afternoon and evening. We must get some discussion groups going, make it a bit lively, then finish up with tea on Sunday. About five-thirty. Let's hope they'll all have homes to go to – it will be quite late enough.' He paused and gave them all a dark, measured look. 'Any questions?' he asked automatically. Naturally there weren't any. No one dared. 'Good! So now it just remains for us to decide who can do what – and when. First of all, can you tell me who *cannot* be available for any particular weekend ...'

The meeting dragged on and on. Emma excused herself after an hour, and so did the little man from the board of Trustees.

'Most interesting,' he muttered in the hall as Emma helped him struggle into his coat. 'Amazing fellow, Voss. Loads of imagination.'

Imagination! Emma felt like calling it something else. And by the time she eventually returned to the sitting room, Louis, Colin and Nicholas were all still in full flood. Laughter drifted beneath the door to greet her. Her uncle was actually sitting on the edge of his chair. Colin and Nicholas were discussing the Chinese influence on Chippendale and they obviously wouldn't stop for ages. It was no good, she would have to offer them all a meal.

The three men seemed in good spirits throughout supper. Finally all the arrangements had been made, and Nicholas said there was really nothing now to stop them going ahead.

'We can begin our advertising campaign in earnest,' he said, passing his empty plate along the line. 'Another couple of weeks should see the alterations completed upstairs, which will give you both,' he said, glancing from Louis to Colin, 'ample time to prepare your series of talks.'

'I've already thought of mine,' said Colin enthusiastically. 'Been sorting it all out during the
evenings. That's why I haven't seen much of you
lately, love,' he added, with a little wink at
Emma.

Nicholas' lips thinned. He remained silent.

'So that seems to be everything settled most
satisfactorily,' said Uncle Louis, sliding gracefully
into the breach. 'Everything, that is, except our
little Emma. I haven't heard anything mentioned
about her part in all this. Are you contemplating
running this little venture, my dear Nicholas,
without her assistance?'

Nicholas looked cross; like a man forced to discuss an unsavoury topic. He looked down the
length of the table at Emma, his fine brows pulled
together, his expression withdrawn, remote; but
when he finally spoke there was a dangerous
undercurrent of passion.

'I would be foolish in the extreme,' he began
quietly, 'if I imagined I didn't need Emma's help.
Of course I do – we all do ...' He appeared to be
speaking to Louis, but Emma knew that her uncle
and Colin needn't have existed. Nicholas was
choosing his words with deliberate care. She could
sense he was really speaking to her alone. 'She
will have complete responsibility for all house-
hold matters,' he continued firmly. 'Housekeep-
ing – catering – engaging extra part-time staff.

Everything of that nature I shall leave in her hands.'

She caught Colin's eyes, he was smiling at her, almost, she thought irritably, as if she was supposed to be pleased at being nothing but a glorified housekeeper. That wasn't in Emma's line at all – and her uncle knew it.

'I'm very pleased, Nicholas, to hear you have us all organised.' Louis began. Now *he* was doing it – this double-talking business. 'And I'm sure it would make everyone's burden less if you didn't have me to worry about. Naturally, I'm anxious to get back to my flat – I can commute quite easily – and I'm sure the extra bedroom will be useful to you.' He helped himself to a slither of Stilton and selected a biscuit. 'If you'll just tell me when you're moving in, my dear boy, then I can make arrangements to move out ...'

Louis moving! Emma nearly fell off her chair. He couldn't. Surely he was joking. He wouldn't really leave her alone in the house with this wretched man.

'Really, my dear Louis, you mustn't let us keep you one moment more than is necessary,' Nicholas purred, quite as silkily as his opponent. 'We're very grateful for all the help you've been these past months ... I'm sure Emma doesn't need me to say ...'

'You're right,' she interrupted briskly. 'I'm

perfectly capable of voicing my own gratitude, and I have done, on more than one occasion. Louis knows perfectly well that I couldn't have managed without him.'

'But you must feel free to get back to your own surroundings, Louis, as soon as you wish,' said Nicholas quickly, as if he didn't want Emma to say anything more. 'I'm more than grateful that you're prepared to help out with my little scheme at weekends, and with Colin organising things so well in town,' he turned and gave one of his rare, beaming smiles to the younger man, 'then there really is no excuse for me to remain in Mayfair beyond this weekend. I'm more than happy to move in on Saturday – if that's all right with everyone.'

'Splendid!' Louis looked quite chuffed. 'Can't say I'm not looking forward to getting back – one's own bits and pieces – you know how it is ...'

'Will that be all right, Emma?' Nicholas asked, when everyone was eventually helping to clear away and they had found themselves alone in the dining room.

Emma collected the table mats and napkins. Nicholas picked up the cruet. They met by the sideboard and there was an awkward moment when their hands brushed together. The homely task they were sharing made Emma feel strangely vulnerable, there was something so normal, so domestic – it simply felt *right* ... She pushed the feeling away – the moment was lost.

'Will what be all right?' she asked, pretending that everything he had said wasn't imprinted on her memory for ever.

'Me moving in on Saturday.' The blue eyes watched her carefully. 'Will it make things difficult?' She was surprised, and curiously pleased, that he had bothered to ask. But then he probably would have asked any housekeeper, and her little warm glow suddenly vanished.

'Of course it's all right.' She shuffled everything into a drawer and closed it. 'You're the boss,' she shrugged brightly. 'There's no need to ask *us* if you can or can't do anything. I'm sure I'm the last person who wants to interfere with any of your plans ...'

'I'm glad to hear it.' His eyes and temper ignited with her expression. 'Because you won't be able to stop me, Emma. Not in my plans for Whitewayes ...' He caught hold of her arm, strong fingers bit into soft flesh, as he continued harshly, 'And you won't be able to stop any of my other plans, either.'

'What other plans?' she demanded. Hadn't he done enough to the house already? What other devastation could he possibly have in mind?

'My other plans for you,' he taunted, his lips

twisting into the semblance of a smile. 'Don't you know they're the most important plans of all?'

There was something decidely menacing in his quiet tone. She struggled to get free, but her useless efforts did nothing more than amuse him.

'You have no right to make any plans for me ...'

'I have *every* right – and I intend making full use of it.' She could tell he was suddenly becoming aware of her; of soft supple limbs, of pliant body. His hands travelled over her possessively in a mixture of censure and caress. Lights danced in his eyes and for a second her own reflected the bright desire she recognised. She heard his faint gasp as his searching eyes discovered her – as if for the first time. The hands around her waist drew her nearer. She was practically certain Nicholas was going to kiss her – and she was absolutely certain that she had never wanted anything more than that in all her life. Excitement touched her soul – it leapt and darted deep within her – but then there was a noise, the sound of footsteps coming down the hall.

Nicholas cursed softly under his breath. They broke away from each other embarrassed, confused; a still-life tableau frozen into immobility as Colin came into the room.

'Is there anything else to take out? he began cheerfully. Then he registered the scene, took stock

of the situation – and Emma could feel slow anger
stir within him.

His eyes sought hers, but she managed to avoid
them. She didn't know why she felt so awkward.
Had anything been about to happen, or had it
been nothing more than her imagination?

But she would never know. The moment was
gone, and Nicholas with it, and Colin was suddenly determined to sweep her into a headlong
round of activity.

'Haven't been seeing enough of you lately,' he
said a few evenings later during a concert in-
terval. The bar was crowded, conversation difficult, Emma smiled up at him and said nothing.
They were jostled away from the counter and
Colin put a large, protective arm around her
shoulders. 'You're sure you don't mind me working for Nicholas Voss?' he said suddenly. 'I
mean – I'll be around quite a bit at weekends.'
He broke off, swirling the ice around his glass,
then hesitant grey eyes smiled down at her.

'Of course I don't mind.' She squeezed his arm
and sipped her Martini. 'I've told you before, it's
your career ...'

'And it's my life?' he interrupted quietly.

'Yes.' Their eyes met. There was no need for
her to say more. Colin sighed and drained his
glass as the little bell rang to summon them all

back into the auditorium.

'It's a pity Louis couldn't come,' Emma chatted gaily as they settled themselves into their seats. 'He loves Brahms – he was sorry to miss it.' Colin didn't seem to be particularly sad at her uncle's absence. His oh-dear-what-a-pity look had them both giggling as the applause once more acknowledged the leader.

'Why couldn't he come?' whispered Colin, as the man bowed and took his place at the front desk of the violins.

'He's moved back to his flat – been coming and going with bits and pieces all day.' The clapping dwindled then resumed again as the conductor strode purposefully on to the platform. The baton was raised, all conversation ceased, but enough had been said to totally end Emma's peace of mind.

For one whole evening she had actually forgotten the new arrangements. Uncle Louis had moved out – Nicholas Voss had moved in. He would be at home – waiting for her at Whitewayes – when she returned.

The Brahms third symphony always had the power to sweep her headlong with its glorious, uplifting exuberance. But this time it wasn't so easy to give herself up to the music. Nicholas came between her and the rich tapestry of sound. How could she cope with him? How could she possibly stop him ruining Whitewayes? Emma stared at the conductor's back, unseeing, for once almost unhearing, without the least idea of which movement they had reached. She wouldn't be able to invite Colin in for coffee – not with Nicholas there . . . She hoped he would understand.

'It's just that it's rather late,' she mumbled, when the time eventually came, and Colin had parked on the gravel drive at the front of the house. 'It's been a lovely evening – a real change – but . . .'

Colin slid his arm along the back of her seat. 'I've enjoyed it too.' She could see his eyes glistening in the dark as he undid the top button of her coat and ran a thumb gently up her neck. His kiss was tender, loving; she responded automatically, touching his cheek, running her fingers into his hair, but nothing happened to her. Nothing at all. No spark, no ignition, just a warm, pleasurable experience. Simply a comfort.

'I must go,' she whispered against his cheek. 'Give me a ring – tell me what's going on. You're right – we haven't been seeing enough of each other.' That was the real trouble, she decided. They were just out of touch. It had been a mistake to get so involved with the house just lately.

Colin drew back reluctantly. 'Emma, you know . . .' he began, but the rest didn't come.

Of course it wouldn't, Emma realised. Because

you had to be reckless to tell someone you loved them – not knowing for certain if they loved you in return. And Colin would never be reckless. She sighed, momentarily wishing that just this once he would be.

The sound of Colin's car was little more than a distant purr when Emma finally tiptoed across the hall. She noticed there was still a light under the sitting room door, but she had no wish to cross swords with Nicholas tonight. She hoped he hadn't heard her come in.

But it was wishful thinking. Halfway up the stairs she heard the door opening and it was impossible to ignore it.

'Ah, good, I thought I heard something. Please don't go up yet. I want a word with you.' She looked reluctant and he seemed to expect it. 'I know it's late – but this is important.' He stood back, holding the door open for her. 'There's something I must discuss with you – and it certainly can't wait until the morning.'

'I really don't see what can be so vital,' said Emma, shrugging out of her coat and following him into the sitting room. It was warm and cosy, with soft lights and a cheerful fire. Music was playing quietly from the stereo, a pile of books and papers surrounded the most comfortable chair, beside which was a glass of brandy. Nicholas Voss certainly knew how to make him-

self at home, and he wasted no time in going
about it.

'A drink?' he offered, almost as if she was going
to need one, and when she shook her head he
strolled across to his chair and picked up his own
glass. For some reason he didn't sit down — so
neither did Emma, and she watched as his eyes
darted from his glass to her face — and to the fire.
There was something menacing, dangerous, lurk-
ing not very far beneath the surface. Emma's
stomach suddenly contracted with fear, as he
began severely, 'I'm afraid, my dear Emma, that
we've come across a sticky problem.'

CHAPTER SIX

'WELL, don't stop there. What's the problem? You'll have to tell me now.' Emma put a brave face on it, but she wasn't feeling very brave.

Nicholas sighed. 'I've had a letter.' He indicated his briefcase as if the offending document was inside, but he appeared to have no intention of showing it to her. 'From the Trustees,' he went on quietly. 'I'm afraid they're not very happy with things as they are ...'

Emma could well believe it. Perhaps someone on the committee had come to their senses at last. 'You mean they're not happy with the weekend courses?' she asked, trying not to gloat.

'What?' He looked surprised that she should even mention them. 'Oh, that! No, Emma.' He frowned and paced the carpet, coming to rest with his back to the fire as she expected. 'It's this situation ...' An expressive hand indicated the room, bereft of any occupants except themselves. 'It's you and I – here alone ...'

'Oh, come on now – this is the twentieth century. You're not suggesting ...' Firelight reflected brilliantly in Emma's eyes as Nicholas stared at her.

'*I*'m not suggesting anything,' he said, coming back to life quickly. Too quickly. There was more to all this than just a few ancient Trustees with Victorian scruples. Emma held her breath as he went on. 'Apparently it's a question of contracts. My contract, to be precise, which doesn't – can't – include you.'

'I've never had a contract,' Emma interrupted. 'I really don't see ...'

'Exactly!' Nicholas' voice was suddenly stronger and she realised how cautious he had sounded before. 'It was your father, Emma, who was appointed by the Trustees. After his death you only remained ...'

'On *sufferance?*' she said for him. 'That's it, isn't it? That's what you're trying to say.' She could suddenly see herself being slid out of position. Everything she had worked for – everything her father had worked for – and all for nothing, because this man had the power to manipulate a board of gullible old men. 'You're trying to get rid of me, aren't you? There's really no need to look so surprised,' she said, trying to laugh. 'It's obviously what you've wanted from the very beginning. If a letter has been sent it's all your doing. Is that why the little man came round the other evening? Poking about, asking me all sorts of questions. I wondered why. If they think this situation is unsuitable,' she went on bitterly, 'it's only because you put the idea into their heads.'

She came and stood directly in front of him, heedless of being so dangerously close. He towered over her and she could feel the tension as he strove for self-control. She should have been warned, but anger rose above commonsense. 'Well, you won't get rid of me as easily as you got rid of Uncle Louis,' she declared haughtily. 'So don't try and intimidate me, Nicholas Voss, because it won't work.' Her chest rose and fell, colour tinged her cheeks, adrenalin pumped through her veins bringing her alive and glowing with determination.

Nicholas matched her passion; his nostrils flared, blue eyes crackled with anger as they swept over her incensed figure. His face was livid and the skin around his lips drained white. For one incredible moment she thought he was going to beat her, so she held her head higher, defiant, daring him almost, yet knowing all the while that he was master of his own emotions. He wouldn't give way — would he? The uncertainty stretched her nerves to a knife edge of fear, her throat felt dry, her heart pounded in her ears — in a moment everything would end in total blackness ...

But it didn't. Nicholas let out his breath in a long, barely audible sigh.

'And you think I would ...' he began slowly, in

a voice a little above a whisper.

'You're ruthless enough to do anything,' Emma responded; shattered now by the strain, yet knowing the danger had passed, for the moment at least.

'You're right – I *am* ruthless.' He paused and looked at her for a long moment. Not with anger, this time, but thoughtfully, his own eyes veiled of emotion. He looked like a man weighing the possibilities, pondering, deciding. But deciding on what? she wondered. 'I know what I want, Emma,' he went on at last. 'And yes, I'm ruthless enough to get it. But whatever you may think, I don't want you to leave – on the contrary, as I said the other day. You are a vital member of the team. Without you ...' he broke off with a shrug. It wasn't exactly a compliment, but it was obviously the nearest he was going to get to one.

Emma wanted to laugh hysterically. 'You've got to admit it's amusing.'

'Is it?' His eyes met hers, then slid away.

'I think so.' She couldn't explain; it was all too complicated. He wanted her to stay for all the wrong reasons. You had to laugh or else you would cry. She felt suddenly deflated. What was the point of staying on – fighting him? If only she hadn't loved him quite so much!

'Of course there is a solution,' Nicholas said quietly. He was looking down at the rug, tapping

one foot lightly. 'There is a way you can stay on –
and keep everyone happy. I presume you *do* want
to stay?' She nodded at once, and he smiled
briefly to himself, believing her acquiescence was
for no other reason than to protect Whitewayes.
'And you're prepared to go to any lengths?'

'Yes.' Her voice shook.

'You're sure?' His was steady.

'Quite sure.'

'Then may I suggest, my dear Emma, that you
marry me?'

Silence stretched on and on between them,
until the little Napoleon ormolu clock delicately
chimed midnight – and the spell was broken.

'You're joking,' she managed to breathe.

'I never joke,' he responded quietly.

'You're crazy, then.'

'No, I'm quite sane.'

'I rather think I'd better sit down.' Emma collapsed into a chair. One day had ended, another
had just begun. How could she survive this one
through to the end when her heart was bursting
with emotion?

'At least you haven't tried to run away this
time.' Nicholas seemed to be attempting to lighten
the atmosphere; for once Emma was grateful to
him. 'I realise this isn't exactly every girl's dream
of a proposal.' He sipped his brandy. 'But then
this wouldn't be everyone's idea of a marriage.

This is my family home as much as it's yours, Emma. And I have no wish to see one of the big Trusts take it over. Whatever you might think, my ideas are good – but, as with any new scheme, the first twelve months will be critical. It's such a short time, really, in such a young life ...'

She could feel him gazing down at the top of her head. There it was again, the difference between them. It was obvious he thought of her as little more than a child. Then why was he even contemplating marrying her? Surely he must feel something?

'That's all I ask, Emma. A year. Just give me a year.' He hesitated and cleared his throat. 'I don't expect – anything – from you. It won't be that kind of relationship.'

'What's supposed to happen at the end of a year?' This was a very curious conversation. Not a bit as she had imagined it in all her dreams.

He shrugged. 'These things are easily arranged nowadays. I wouldn't keep you against your will, Emma. You would be quite free if you wanted to go – after a year.'

There was something in his tone which told her she wouldn't be free *during* the year. While she was his wife certain things would be expected – a certain standard would have to be maintained. She would have to act the role fully for the benefit of outsiders. Imagine being his wife ... yet not sharing his bed. Imagine him even suggesting it. It just went to prove how much he certainly didn't love her.

'You'll have to let me think about it,' she managed to say eventually.

He seemed to expect as much. 'But don't keep me waiting long, Emma.' There was an odd catch in his voice which made her look up at him quickly. 'I mean, the Trustees,' he began hesitantly, 'they will have to be informed.'

'Of course.' Emma struggled to her feet. 'I'll see you in the morning, Nicholas,' she said, while he remained silent, standing in front of the fire as she walked out of the room quietly. She could hear no sound of movement from the room behind her as she leant back against the door and closed her eyes. What an ordeal. And she had survived it. Now it was just a question of surviving for ever.

Tonight the curving marble stairs had never seemed so long as Emma's feet echoed slowly and thoughtfully upwards. At the top of the stairs was the portrait of the first mistress of Whitewayes, her dark curls delicately etched against her cheek; the white dress simple, flimsy, the high sash accentuating the roundness of her figure. And there was the pendant. A love token, it had been, from the man who had given her so much, but whom she could never call her own.

It was a sad story, Emma remembered. They had been so very much in love, but for some reason she couldn't marry her lover, yet he had built and installed her in this house. And for propriety's sake an unquestioning husband had been found.

Emma paused on the stairs, staring up at her ancestor. And as Mrs. Nicholas Voss, she, Emma, would be as near to becoming mistress of White-wayes as anyone could be nowadays. And was she, too, doomed to be as unlucky in love as this other woman? Maybe the house was cursed, Emma smiled to herself and continued along the landing. She was just being fanciful, it was probably tiredness, but now that she was no longer with Nicholas, her brain began to tick over. Would a man marry someone for the sake of an estate? He didn't have anything to gain personally. In fact, he would have more to gain — more wealth and position — if he were to marry Gail Weston.

Then why didn't he? Had Emma mistaken the signs of love when he had brought the rich widow to Whitewayes? And if he didn't love Gail could she really make him love herself in as many days as there were in a year? Because that was the truth, wasn't it? Emma undressed slowly and thoughtfully. If she said 'yes' and agreed to marry Nicholas, it would be a delusion to suppose it would be for any other reason than to win his love.

But it couldn't be done — could it? He would never really love her — would he? Questions and hope, despair and fleeting glimpses of a magical existence tormented Emma until finally she gave up all thought of sleep.

There was another problem as well, she realised some time during the night. Marriage to Nicholas would mean giving him support in this venture — if she wanted him to love her. But he was about to do everything her father had feared most. Would the National Trust, or someone like them, really have to take over if this scheme didn't work? Was it really essential for her to stay? Maybe she should have a word with Uncle Louis. She sighed, turning over and thumping her pillow. But what was the point? She was just looking for excuses; any other reason to marry Nicholas except the real reason — the simple fact that she loved him. It would be far better to be married to him, whatever the conditions, than to be out of his life for ever. It was an uneasy feeling to discover that she didn't have the strength of spirit to say 'no'.

Nicholas heard the acceptance of his proposal with calm dignity.

'... and I've given it a lot of thought,' Emma stumbled on, at breakfast next morning, 'and I'm sure you are right. The estate must come first. And after all,' she managed to raise her eyes to his face, 'what's a year?' she said brightly. 'Only three hundred and sixty-five days.' Was that really all it was? It seemed an extremely short time to achieve so much.

'I'm sure you've made the right decision. I'll organise a special licence; there's little point in delaying things longer than is necessary?' It was a question, so she nodded her agreement. 'Right then.' He pushed back his empty plate and stood up. 'I've got a lot of paperwork to do.' For the first time she noticed how tired he looked. 'I'm quite prepared to hold the fort here – if you want to go into town,' he shrugged, 'for any reason.'

'It's Sunday.'

'I thought you might like to see – Louis.'

She shook her head, determined not to appear the starry-eyed young bride. 'Things sometimes get pretty hectic on a Sunday. I'd better stay. I can do anything I want tomorrow. We're closed on a Monday,' she reminded him. 'It's my day off.'

'As you please.' He took a few bits and pieces over to the sink. She couldn't see his face, but the set of his shoulders was stiff – uncompromising. There was something he wasn't very pleased about.

Emma remained at the table long after he had

gone. She chewed the toast round and round, her mind still foggy – still in a state of shock at the situation she had got herself into. Was it really going to happen? What on earth would Louis say? Come to that ... She swallowed and the crumbs almost choked her. Come to that, what on earth would *Colin* say?

'I just don't believe it,' was his very natural response when she called in at the Mayfair shop during Monday lunch time. 'Emma, we have to talk. Have you eaten? Good, I know a little place around the corner ...'

'I'm sure it must seem all rather sudden,' Emma began, picking her way half-heartedly through a salad. Colin was gazing at her intently from the other side of the little table. The restaurant was crowded, noisy, not exactly the right place for a private *tête-à-tête*. 'But I've known Nicholas a long time,' she tried again. 'We were very close – once.'

'And he just comes waltzing back into your life and thinks he'll take up where he left off?'

'It isn't like that.'

'No?' It was only to be expected that Colin should feel hurt. Emma hadn't imagined that this was going to be easy. 'Oh, I don't blame you, Emma.' He laid down his knife and fork with a clatter, for once not exactly enthusiastic about his food. 'I just hope you'll be happy,' he said, trying to smile.

Happy? What was happy? For the next three weeks Emma tried not to think about the word. At times she would be deliriously happy. She was going to be Nicholas' wife, and he had insisted on a white wedding. There were things to buy and Uncle Louis to advise on this or that headdress.

'And a nightgown and negligee, my dear,' he had instructed, and Emma had blushed and tried to say no, but he had insisted.

Such hectic days, made longer by the approaching spring. March arrived, daffodils nodded in the park and Emma continued to play the part of a happy young bride for everyone else's benefit. Sometimes it was easy to forget it was only make-believe. Returning to Whitewayes after one shopping expedition, she met Nicholas in the hall. It was after four – they had the house to themselves, it seemed suddenly so peaceful with sunlight streaming in through the tall, stained glass windows.

'I've had the most wonderful good fortune,' said Emma, manoeuvring herself and her boxes past Nicholas. 'The most beautiful dress – just the right length ... with pearls ...'

'Careful,' he chided softly, 'you're not supposed to tell me.' And they had both laughed, Nicholas' eyes had laughed too, but Emma was halfway up the stairs before she realised it. She glanced back down to the hall quickly, hoping to see him standing there, looking up. But he wasn't, he was nowhere in sight. It hadn't meant anything — it had just been an accident. A cloud passed over the sun and the hallway dimmed.

'My dear, you look delightful — I'm the proudest of uncles.' Louis kissed her on both cheeks, then shook Nicholas by the hand. 'You have a lovely wife — take care of her,' he suggested wisely. Then he moved on, making way for the next guest.

It was over — the reception was about to begin. Emma blinked and smiled automatically. This was the craziest day of her life — or was she simply dreaming?

But of course it couldn't be a dream; here was everyone she knew, family, friends, Colin — yes, Colin had come. That was sweet of him. And here was Nicholas beside her again, looking absolutely devastating in his formal morning suit, his eyes bluer than ever as he laughed and smiled at the quiet comments whispered in his ear.

'It was only supposed to be a quiet family affair,' she said to Colin, when they both found themselves reaching for a vol-au-vent. 'Nicholas suggested having the reception in the ballroom, and I must admit it's rather lovely,' she added, looking around the lofty room with its row of french windows and view of the park. 'But I didn't imagine it would be quite so full of people.'

'You're a popular couple.' Colin's eyes slid away from hers. She could tell he was making a conscious effort not to gaze at her adoringly. 'What's the matter?' His concern, nevertheless, was immediate. 'Having trouble? That thing looks a bit vicious.'

'It is.' Emma tried to wriggle the headdress into a more comfortable position, but a regiment of pins anchored it firmly in place. She already had the niggling of a headache. 'I think I'm going to have to take it off. The hairdresser fixed it on about ten o'clock this morning. Do you think anyone will miss me if I slip upstairs?'

Colin had tried to joke about guarding her secret to the death, and Emma was still smiling when she reached her room and sat down on the dressing table stool. Surely he couldn't be *so* brokenhearted if he could come to the wedding? Perhaps he had just been in love with the idea of love.

Emma stared into the oval mirror hanging on the wall – and saw her image staring back. It really was a lovely dress. Simple, fitted, with long narrow sleeves and a lowish square neck. Tiny pearls had been sewn on to the bodice and Louis had given her a matching string to wear around her neck. The veil showered behind her, accentuating her cap of dark hair. A pixie, Nicholas used to call her. But she didn't look like a pixie today. Today she was a bride ... Emma smiled ruefully and remembered her headache. Bride or no bride, the headdress would have to go.

It was a slow, painful operation. Only half the pins had been taken out when there was a gentle tap on her door. Before she had time to call out, the door opened and warmth stirred within her as she gazed into the mirror – and saw Nicholas.

CHAPTER SEVEN

'I saw you slip away. Is anything the matter? We can't have the bride deserting her own reception.' Nicholas closed the door and came into the room slowly. Emma was alone with her husband for the first time.

She watched him come towards her in the mirror; his jacket smoothed over broad shoulders and its quiet formality belying the vibrant strength and determination of the man beneath.

He came and stood directly behind her, and the fingers in her hair trembled a little as she attempted to pull out another pin.

'Is it hurting?' His voice was almost gentle, and he frowned when she nodded. Then his own fingers were moving in her hair and her hands drifted helplessly downwards.

He removed the veil with great care and Emma sighed with relief as he shook it free and laid it on her bed.

'Headache?' he asked, their eyes meeting in the mirror, and then he came behind her again, laying cool fingers on her temples and urging her to lean back against him.

For a moment she was tense, embarrassed by such intimacy, but then her eyes closed and she let everything drift into the distance except the wonderful sensation of long, supple fingers easing away discomfort. His hands moved down her neck and along delicate shoulders. His thumbs teased gentle circles at the top of her spine, and without thinking, she rolled her head backwards displaying a long column of slender white neck. She felt him tremble and stir to life against her.

Instinct made Emma stay perfectly still as his hands caressed her neck moving slowly up to her chin – then down again. His other hand explored her cheek – the line of her jaw – like a connoisseur carefully handling fine porcelain.

Emma knew she wouldn't be able to stay still much longer. If only she could turn and bury her face against him, if only she could feel his arms lovingly lift her up so that she could be kissed – made love to ... A dull longing throbbed within her. But she made no move; to show her feelings, just once, would be to lose all self-respect. Nicholas might even pity her. Emma couldn't think of anything more intolerable.

'Your self-control does you credit, madam wife,' said Nicholas suddenly. His voice was as caustic as his hands were smooth, and Emma's eyes flew open. As she gazed up into a face as cold and bitter as a winter wind, he added con-

temptuously, 'Don't worry, I have no intention
of claiming my nuptial rights. You must indeed
love this house very much!' He stood away from
her and Emma picked up the hairbrush, it was
something to do with her hands. 'We'd better go
down together,' he said, waiting for her by the
door. 'Now that you're my wife you'd better start
playing the part.'

They walked side by side down the wide marble
staircase, Nicholas lightly holding her elbow – a
perfect picture of married bliss.

The front door bell rang as they reached the
bottom and Nicholas let go of her arm and went
to open it, and his fixed smile changed to one of
genuine pleasure when he recognised the newcomer.

'Darling, I'm so late – have I missed everything? I tried to get away earlier – it was such a
bore ...'

Nicholas automatically offered his cheek to
be kissed. 'I'd almost given you up,' he said
sadly. 'No, of course you haven't missed anything.'

Emma hung back in the shadows, closing her
eyes momentarily and sighing. Gail Weston. Trust
her to turn up, that was all she needed.

'How delightful ...' came the greeting, and
Emma stepped forward to meet the latest guest.
'What a *lovely* dress!' Gail enthused even more.

'Nicholas darling, you really do have a charming little wife. I do hope you know how to look after her!'

Nicholas led Gail towards the ballroom, inclining his head and murmuring a reply in her ear. Emma couldn't catch what he said, but she watched as they both laughed seductively with all the ease and intimacy of very close friends.

She didn't hurry after them as they passed the library without a glance; each absorbed with the other, she guessed. But when Emma reached the library she noticed the door was open and a sound of movement came from inside. Perhaps one of the children had escaped parental control – there were some valuable books on the shelves – Emma went inside to check.

'Was that Mrs. Weston I heard arriving?' It was Colin inside, flicking through a leather-bound volume. There was a gap on the shelf where it should have been, Emma was surprised she even noticed.

'She got held up,' she explained, coming into the room and wandering over to the window. There were a few people strolling around the park, but Emma was glad it had been agreed to close the house for the weekend. Today Whitewayes could be a real home celebrating a family wedding. *Celebrating!* That was a laugh. Emma resolutely turned back to Colin.

'Nicholas said I could borrow it.' He closed the book and put it on the the desk. 'Thought I'd get it while I remembered — brain like a sieve ...' She nodded and he plunged his hands into tight pockets and paced about self-consciously. 'You'd have thought she would have kept away today of all days,' he said crossly, and Emma was surprised to hear gentle Colin speak so vehemently.

She totally agreed with him, but perhaps now was the time to begin playing the act of a loving — confident — young wife.

'It's only natural — they've been friends for years. I think it was very good of her to come in the circumstances.'

Colin looked puzzled. Emma was reminded of their own parallel relationship, and wished she had said nothing.

'I mean,' she stumbled on in embarrassment, 'perhaps she'd even hoped to marry Nicholas herself.' Heavens! This was getting worse. 'I mean, they are — were — free to marry,' she added firmly, and that had been the one glimmer of hope in all this business. If Nicholas had truly loved Gail he wouldn't — couldn't — have married Emma. Not for Whitewayes — not even for the estate. Surely no man could be so ruthless — nor any woman understand such action. They couldn't have loved each other totally. Emma's eyes pleaded for Colin to understand.

There was silence in the room for a long time as he slowly returned to the desk and perched on the edge. He gazed at her thoughtfully as she stood framed by the tall window; the plain, long dress accentuating the fairness of her skin, the delicacy of her figure. She looked fragile, vulnerable, belonging to another age, as if she had stepped down from one of the portraits in the gallery.

'You don't know, do you?' he said eventually, and then the quietness closed around them again. Somewhere in the house the reception was in full swing, but it had no meaning – no reality – in here.

Colin was staring at her again, seeing the wedding dress, her ring ... She could tell which way his mind was travelling. 'Know what?' she prompted, steering him away from dangerous ground.

He blinked and drew a deep breath, smiling briefly down at the floor before looking up at her again, this time quite seriously.

'I guess you don't – didn't – realise that Gail wasn't free to marry Nicholas ...'

'*Wasn't* free?' Emma heard herself say.

'Legally free, yes,' Colin said quickly. 'But her husband, her late husband, made a bit of a tight will. She has everything, control of the business, et cetera, for as long as she remains unmarried ...'

'And if she should remarry?' Emma asked lightly.

Colin passed a finger across his throat. 'She just gets the house and an allowance, so the story goes. All the rest goes to the old boy's son. Apparently her husband was married before, had a grown-up family. I don't know much about it – just what I've heard ...'

'It's enough!' If Emma could have moved she would have sunk into a chair, but for once she doubted the power of her legs. 'It's a sad story ...' she murmured.

Colin was watching her carefully. 'Very sad.'

'But I still think she wouldn't have come if she was suffering from a broken heart. A woman wouldn't, Colin, really,' Emma tried to convince him. 'If it was me I would want to keep well out of the way.' Unless she knew it was all a plan, that the marriage meant absolutely nothing to Nicholas ... But Emma kept this last, treacherous thought to herself.

'I'm sure you're right.' Colin smiled cheerfully and picked up the book. 'Come on, you're missing the party.' He crossed to the window and gave her a hug, kissing her on the top of her head in a very brotherly fashion, and just for a second

Emma allowed herself the comfort of resting her forehead against his broad chest. He gently stroked her hair with his big hands and she totally relaxed, feeling closer to him than she ever had before. Now that she was married one side of their relationship had stopped, but they were still left with a genuine regard for each other. It was nice to have a friend in such troubled times.

'Is your headache still very bad, my dear?' Nicholas' voice was icy as he came into the room and closed the door. 'Thank you for looking after my wife so diligently,' he said to Colin, as she broke awkwardly away from him. 'If it's that bad, my dear, I should go and lie down,' he said, striding across the room and putting a possessive arm around her shoulders. 'It's all the tensions of the day — everyone will understand.' His smile was bright, the tone of his voice lightened to the conversational, but she could feel anger bubbling inside him as he pretended to kiss her affectionately.

She tried to look at Colin, to say she was sorry, that it was all right — but he wasn't looking her way. In fact, he really wasn't looking at anything except the bookcase — the desk — and now a chair. He looked so embarrassed, if only she could tell him there was no need.

Emma dismissed her headache, returning with

Nicholas to the ballroom and her guests, and if any of them had noticed her absence they made no comment. Her reappearance with Nicholas said all they needed to know.

By mid-afternoon, when the caterers were discreetly tidying up and most of the guests had drifted away, Emma really did have a dreadful headache. Her mouth felt dry, there hadn't been time to do more than nibble a few bits and pieces. If only she could have a quiet cup of tea! Now that the reception was almost over another problem began to present itself. What was going to happen when everyone had gone and she and Nicholas had Whitewayes to themselves? Perhaps Uncle Louis and Colin would stay for tea. Emma smiled inside, imagining her uncle's reaction and decided not to invite them. She would have to take tea alone with her husband. There would be no getting out of it.

Husband! Emma practised the unfamiliar word in her vocabulary. Yes, he was now, and she glanced at the tall, dark man by her side. He had his hand on the smooth silk of her sleeve as he laughed and joked with one of the guests. But Emma knew his good humour was nothing but facade. He was very, very angry about finding her with Colin. And that was something else she couldn't get away with. Sooner or later the hammer would fall ...

The last guest kept Nicholas talking out in the car park for ages, so Emma made her escape upstairs. She wanted to get out of the dress and into something that would make her feel less vulnerable. But Nicholas didn't give her time. She was only halfway out of her wedding dress, hopping about awkwardly on one foot, when he came marching into her bedroom. He hadn't even allowed her the courtesy of knocking.

'You're very eager to remove the vestments of marriage,' he said wryly. 'What's the matter, Emma, do they burn your skin?' He made no move to help as she stumbled about, trying not to crush what was, after all, a very beautiful dress.

'The party's over, as they say.' She stood facing him with the dress in her arms. Now it was empty, lifeless, like the hollowness of their marriage. 'I've played my part,' she went on bitterly, 'the act is over for today.'

'Act? Hah!' He threw back his head and gave a mirthless laugh. 'If you imagine I shall tolerate ...' He broke off, his eyes blazing with the anger he had managed, up till now, to contain. Then he took the dress from her, running large expressive hands over the smooth silk and delicately embroidered pearls. 'Such a beautiful dress,' he acknowledged quietly. Then, without caring, he tossed it on to her bed. It fell beside the veil, both of them meaningless trappings. 'And such a beautiful bride,' he went on severely, his eyes slowly exploring Emma in her long, frilly half-slip and lacy bra. 'What a pity the bride doesn't know how to behave like a wife,' he breathed, 'and oh, what a temptation to teach her exactly how to! Shall I, Emma?' Before she could stop him he had pulled her close, pinning her arms behind her back when she struggled, and keeping her wrists locked together with just one of his hands.

'We made an agreement,' she snapped, struggling again, but that only seemed to make him worse.

'Exactly! And that agreement was that you should behave like my wife – and I do not allow my wife to conduct herself in such a manner.'

'I don't know what you're talking about,' Emma lied.

'You want me to tell you? To explain word for word?' Nicholas was losing his concentration. Gradually, it seemed, the situation in the library was becoming less important to him. Excitement was replacing anger in his eyes and Emma's heartbeat responded to match it. 'You don't actually imagine yourself in *love* with Colin Prentice,' he said eventually, and there was such amazement in his voice that it made Emma see red.

'And what if I am?' she declared righteously. 'It's no concern of yours. I'm allowed to love whom I choose ...'

'Not in this house – not in *any* house,' he practically roared. 'Not for a year. That was our agreement, Emma, and I shall remind you of it – daily if necessary. Don't let anything like that happen again.'

She had nearly reached screaming point too. If only he would let her go, if only she wasn't so completely aware of every inch of him against her.

'You can stop me seeing people,' she managed to say, 'you can even lock me up. But you can't stop me thinking about him. So there's no point in you even trying.'

The fingers around her wrists clasped even tighter. She cried out, but he took no notice.

'I could make you forget your own name,' Nicholas whispered menacingly, and she tried to pull away, but he only laughed. 'That's right, Emma, struggle. Make it a good fight ...' He only needed one hand to hold her prisoner, so he lowered his other to her thigh. Gentle strokes, up and down, made more sensuous by her silky petticoat. Emma bit her lip despairingly, as he watched for her reaction. 'Shall I, Emma?' he taunted, 'shall I make you forget?' Now his hand was snaking upwards, finding her waist, the smooth skin of her midriff, then closing gently, but firmly, over the soft lacy bra.

Emma's moan was trapped as his mouth covered hers. The kiss went on and on, in time with the rhythmic movement on her breast, in time with the steady urging of his body – in time with the blood richly throbbing through her veins. Somewhere in the midst of it all, Emma slipped beyond the point of resistance. Her desire for Nicholas became life itself – and love's fulfilment as necessary to her as the air she breathed.

Now he was pulling away from her, even as she murmured his name. But it was only a whisper and he didn't hear.

'Do you believe me now?' he asked, every muscle in his face rigid. 'Do you imagine it would be like this with anyone else?'

Only now did Emma remember that he had been teaching her a lesson. Proving a theory; making her forget Colin and her own name. He had been right – he had succeeded. She could have cried with humiliation that there had been nothing more for him than that.

She stared back at him wildly, knowing she had to think of something really dreadful to say. Something that would hurt him as much as he had hurt her.

'Yes, you've certainly proved it,' she announced haughtily, 'proved what *you* want, at any rate!'

And to her own amazement, and Nicholas' absolute astonishment, she stepped out of her petticoat and hose. 'Your nuptial rights, I believe you called it, this afternoon,' she went on, practically lost now. Not really knowing what she was saying, much less what she was doing. And with trembling fingers she finally undid her bra and let it slip to the floor. 'Well, go ahead,' she offered, her eyes looking enormous, frightened, like a scared rabbit. 'With someone as experienced as you I might even enjoy it.'

Nicholas looked as if he had been slapped in the face. She knew she had insulted him beyond redemption, and she held her breath as his eyes devoured her. She was all smooth and fair, with simple curves – delicate, enticing, like her lacy pants and softly rounded breasts. But her eyes were somehow flashing with hatred and her mouth was set in a firm line of disgust. Her performance should have won her an Oscar.

He didn't move. Emma was suddenly afraid that he would walk out, so she laughed, tempting him even more, even daring to hope he would accept the challenge.

'I do not require a sacrificial lamb,' he said after a very long time. His face was white with rage, his lips two thin lines, his brows welded together with disapproving straightness. 'A man needs a woman, Emma, a warm, mature lover.

Not a silly little girl who doesn't even know her own mind.'

He left her quickly, practically slamming the door in her face, and Emma stared at the empty space in the room without him.

It had worked. How clever she was! But it didn't feel like it. Everything felt dreadful, and she threw herself on to the bed and cried inconsolable tears into her wedding dress and veil.

CHAPTER EIGHT

'MRS. VOSS, I was speaking to your husband ...'
'Such a splendid weekend, Mrs. Voss ...' 'Delightful, Mrs. Voss, we've enjoyed every minute
...' If nothing else, over the next month, Emma
became used to the title of marriage.

The first few courses had unleashed the in-
evitable teething troubles, but these had been
overcome with ingenuity and quick thinking,
when any member of the team was prepared to
do anything. Emma had imagined that their
greatest problem would be opening to the public
as usual between ten and four. How would the
guests react? she had wondered. Surely the
visitors would resent part of the house being
closed ... But Nicholas had arranged a compro-
mise. Only two of the smaller reception rooms
were 'off limits' to the public; who neither missed
them nor complained. And the guests, for the
most part, were kept busy with talks and discus-
sions, and if they came across anyone else as they
trotted from one place to another, they seemed
to enjoy their exalted status of being allowed to
pass beyond the gold-corded barriers. But no one

at all was allowed to pass behind the sitting room door marked 'private'.

And now, on the fifth Friday afternoon since her marriage, Emma wandered down the stairs, lingering to enjoy the peacefulness of the house and the low sun slanting through the stained glass windows. It was a little before five, only a few precious hours remained until the weekend guests arrived. This would be the most tranquil tea until Monday.

The trolley had already been wheeled into the sitting room. That was one advantage of having extra part-time help in the kitchen. The two catering students who were already giving White-wayes the reputation of good cuisine, began their weekend session in time to serve Friday tea.

'I'm glad I waited for you.' Louis refolded his paper and smiled vaguely at Emma. He did a lot of things vaguely these days, she had noticed. He didn't talk to her any more, yet you couldn't say he was unhappy. She handed him his cup and passed a macaroon.

'Is Nicholas coming?' he asked, still staring down at his plate.

Emma shrugged. 'He knows the time. But I think he's in the office – juggling the accounts,' she finished jokingly, but Louis wouldn't have missed the cutting edge beneath the words.

'We've had a good write-up,' said Louis after

a while, nodding down to the local newspaper lying at his feet. 'The Trustees are very pleased with things so far, although of course it's early days yet.'

'Don't talk to me about the Trustees,' Emma interrupted smartly. Sometimes it was easy to forget the falseness of her situation, sometimes she could smile and drift around the house pretending she really was Mrs. Voss. But not with Uncle Louis here, all stiff and unnatural, never asking all those questions or making little innuendoes, like all newly married couples had to bear. It was almost as if he knew ... But of course he didn't. No one did. But it was at times like this, feeling insecure and alone, that Emma wished the board of Trustees had not been such doddering old fools. And that Nicholas had not been so ruthless as to make her pay the price of his success.

'Louis, were things really so very bad?' she said eventually. 'Was there any danger that we might be sold out to one of the big Trusts?'

'A very great danger,' he said, picking up his newspaper once more. 'We must be thankful that Nicholas could persuade them to delay their decision for a year.'

'A year?' It wasn't the first time she had heard those words spoken.

'We're still on borrowed time,' he said, as if

he was reminding her of something she was supposed to know. 'Nicholas may have found a way to save things – and we all hope he has – but he has to get the results within a year. It's all they would agree to.'

Emma stared thoughtfully into the empty grate. It was a warm day, even for April, and she realised two months of Nicholas' year had already flown.

'I'm going to take the dog for a walk,' she announced, leaping to her feet suddenly and causing Uncle Louis to drop his paper in alarm. 'I'll leave the trolley in case Nicholas comes down,' she said brightly, deciding to go out through one of the french windows.

The gardener's spaniel bitch seemed as pleased as Emma to be able to resume their afternoon rambles. Most of the puppies had gone now, and the couple that remained no longer needed, or received, the maternal instincts of their mother. Bess, herself still only two, scurried ahead of Emma, busily sniffing in the undergrowth and rediscovering her favourite nooks and corners.

They wandered down to the lake first and Emma stared across the still expanse of deep green water, towards the pavilion. It was old and tatty now, but for a second she was suddenly swept back to childhood, long before her father had come here to work, in the days when they used to give open-air concerts. There had been

floodlighting then, unobtrusive, hidden in the
trees, and Emma had sat on the sloping lawn on
a warm summer night, thrilled with the spectacle
of almost magical charm – the dark, surrounding
trees, the bright pavilion filled with men in black
jackets and dazzling white shirt fronts. There had
been perhaps two hundred other people sitting all
around her, half of them laughing, excited – the
other half as mistily awed as herself. But all had
stilled to silence as the conductor had walked on
to the platform. Emma could still remember seeing his reflection in the cool, still waters, and her
childish mind had been surprised and disappointed
not to be able to see the reflection of such sweet,
clear music.

Now, instead of music, it was a hammering and
banging about that shattered such a pleasant
memory. Intrigued, Emma disappeared into the
wood and came out on the far shore of the lake.
The path up to the pavilion was narrow, over-
grown, yet someone had obviously walked along
here before her.

It was Nicholas. For a moment she stared at
him in amazement. She had imagined it would be
a workman, or even the gardener having a bit of
a sort out. But nothing had prepared her for the
sight of Nicholas heaving aside planks of timber,
broken chairs, and an old faded awning that had
once been a bright blue and white stripe.

'I thought you were indoors — in the office,' was all she could think to say, when he suddenly swung round and saw her. He was still wearing the fawn trousers and brown suede jacket that he had been wearing all day, and she noticed he was handling everything carefully, keeping it away from him. He obviously hadn't intended pulling the place to pieces. It seemed almost as if he came for a stroll and chanced upon the place.

'The roof's not too bad at all,' he said, gazing upwards and brushing his hands together. He was standing up on the platform, a good two feet above her, but as Emma looked upwards her eyes rose no further than his face. He really was extraordinarily handsome, so strong and capable. There was such presence, such resolution, in his strong, masterful face and body.

He jumped down lightly to the ground, running fingers through his thick dark hair; yet he seemed preoccupied, miles away. This chance meeting held no importance for such a busy man. Emma called Bess, and all three of them began to amble back down the dark, overhanging path.

Now she had a chance to secretly study her husband as she trailed after him. It all seemed so long ago now; their wedding day. But its memory didn't have to return, it remained with her always. It was the day-to-day intrusion that seemed more like a dream. And it wasn't the church or reception that Emma was always recalling, but that brief, passionate encounter when she had offered herself so completely – and he had rejected her.

There had been nothing in his behaviour, since then, even to suggest that he remembered the event; but lately, this past week or so, his cool aloofness, his air of detachment, had somehow been subtly altering.

She watched him now, moving back branches for her to duck under, pointing out a muddy patch and calling Bess as the dog wandered off. They had somehow been spending more time in each other's company. Chance meetings, like this one; or was it really chance? And Nicholas had become brooding, intense; sometimes she would catch him watching her, and at those times his eyes would be mysterious, unfathomable, and they would send her heart racing ...

'It would take a lot of work to lick it into shape,' said Nicholas suddenly, turning as the narrow track reached the wood. Now they could walk side by side, and she stared at him stupidly. 'The pavilion.' He seemed amused by her bewilderment. 'There's nothing wrong structurally, nothing that a fresh coat of paint and a few patches wouldn't put right.'

Emma told him about the concerts when she was a child. 'Those were lovely summer evenings,' she reminisced, rubbing her arms that were chilly out of the sun's warmth. 'When summers were really summers ...' she went on, realising, too late, that she sounded like her father or Uncle Louis talking.

She glanced quickly at the man who was her husband, cursing herself for sounding so naïve. Nicholas said nothing, but his lips twisted into the taunting semblance of a smile. 'And you've lived so very many summers,' his brilliant eyes flashed silently, and Emma was reduced to the confusion of a schoolgirl.

The walk through the wood was short and silent. 'I have to take Bess back,' Emma said brightly, when they had reached the lawn. Without waiting for him to speak or accompany her she strode off, calling to the spaniel, and out of the corner of her eye she was aware that Nicholas was walking towards the house. 'Oh, what's the point – he doesn't want you – you're not his type ...' Bess turned inquisitive eyes upwards at the sound of her voice. 'It's all right, I should have more sense than to care,' Emma told the bewildered dog. But she did care. She cared very much – and it hurt.

Emma had stayed at the lodge longer than she had intended. The two remaining puppies had to be cuddled, the latest crisis in the cafeteria discussed with the gardener's wife, who had also read the newspaper report and seemed as enthusiastic about it all as Louis.

Now, realising it must be nearly six o'clock, Emma hurried back across the lawn. The warmth had gone out of the day, but the sinking sun was sending flaming colour to the west-facing windows of Whitewayes. The house looked warm and mellow, and Emma felt a similar glow that she was still part of it all. If Uncle Louis was right – if Nicholas was right – and these courses were essential, then maybe next year they could extend their range to include arts and crafts. Weaving, pottery, dying. There were lots of outbuildings that could be utilised, much more room in the house for bedrooms. It could be great fun...

As she neared the house Emma was suddenly pulled from her reverie by the sight of two figures watching her through the sitting room windows. There was Nicholas, tall, dark and imperious. And a head shorter, Louis, silver-haired, elegant, almost Edwardian ... and there was something in the stance of the two men that made it clear they had been discussing her.

Nicholas opened the door as she came nearer, glancing down at her bright check shirt and blue cord jeans.

'I'm glad you've come now,' he said, as the little clock began to chime. 'Time's getting on – it's six o'clock ...' the rest was left unsaid.

But Emma knew exactly what he left unsaid.

The weekend guests would be arriving at any time and she was hardly in a fit state to meet them.

'It's all right. I'm going upstairs to change now, it won't take me long.' His face tightened and he looked quickly at Louis, but Emma didn't wait to hear what her uncle had to say.

Cheek! Does he imagine I'd play the part of his precious wife looking like a cowgirl? she thought marching out of the sitting room and slamming the door. If he thought she was nothing but an eighteen-year-old schoolgirl then she might as well start acting like one.

Colin stopped suddenly on the stairs. Because of the noise? Or the look on Emma's face? She couldn't be sure which.

'You're early,' she said, trying to find her normal voice, but it was already too late. Colin knew there was something wrong.

'I'm not staying,' he explained, turning round and retracing his steps, and Emma followed him. 'I came over as soon as I closed the shop – want to get a few bits sorted out for my talk tomorrow morning.' He glanced down at her uncertainly. 'I was just coming to find someone to give me a hand.'

'I'm ready for anything,' she said brightly, spreading her hands.

'You're certainly dressed for anything,' said Colin, unconsciously touching a raw spot. 'But

it's just what I need for a spot of furniture removing.'

The little Georgian sofa-table was one of Whitewayes recent acquisitions, Nicholas had come
across it somewhere out of town, and Colin had
spent many hours restoring it to its former charm.
It was probably destined for the Mayfair shop,
but in the meantime everyone was having the
pleasure of it. Now, they closed down the two
small flaps at each end, removed the drawers for
safety, and carefully manoeuvred the table from
the workroom and out on to the landing.

'So it's tables this week, is it?' she chatted, as
they carried it downstairs and into the music
room, where Colin was scheduled to give his talk.
'I've got a lovely little dressing table in my room,
with a top in two halves, that opens sideways.
It's Sheraton – would you like to borrow it for
tomorrow? It won't take me two ticks to clear it
out.'

Colin nodded enthusiastically, and when the
sofa-table was in place and the chairs in the music
room arranged to advantage for his talk, they
raced back upstairs and Emma led the way to her
room.

'Nice,' Colin nodded appreciatively; his experienced eyes running over the neat, clean line, the
square tapered legs and rich bands of satinwood.

'Look, I'll clear it out later and get Nicholas

to help me carry it down.' Emma was conscious of the time slipping by – and of the two men waiting for her downstairs. 'Only I must fly now,' she bustled on, practically pushing Colin out of the room. 'I'll see to it all – don't worry.'

Colin pottered along the corridor to collect the sofa-table drawers, and Emma quickly stripped off and shrugged into her dressing-gown. Ten minutes, that was all she needed, and then she would look as respectable as a dowager at a garden party.

She had to pass the little workroom on the way to the bathroom, the door was still open and Colin appeared to be standing in the middle of the floor gazing into space.

'Is anything the matter?'

He turned quickly and looked towards the door. He looked bemused, disbelieving; simply at a loss for words.

'No, no, just daydreaming.' He picked up the drawers and she closed the door for him as he came out on to the landing. 'See you tomorrow, then,' he murmured, still somewhere away with the fairies, and Emma smiled indulgently as she raced into the bathroom and hurried under the shower.

She had no more time to think of Colin or her promise until, a little before midnight, she was back in her room again, undressed and ready for bed. As she tucked her toes under the sheets her eyes fell upon the dressing table. Damn! It was no good, there wouldn't be time in the morning, and she dragged herself wearily out of bed again.

She was arranging bottles and jars on the top of the chest of drawers when there was a brief knock on the door and in true pre-emptive fashion Nicholas strode quickly into the room. She didn't have time to say 'go away' — even if she had wanted to.

Nicholas was ready for bed as well, but his hair was still wet from a shower, his feet were bare, and he was only wearing the shortie silk dressing-gown she had seen on a couple of occasions. It was loosely tied, she could see dark hairs curling across a chest that still looked a bit damp. Her imagination began to play tricks. She wished she could reach out and touch him, draw him against her and feel the hard toughness beneath the silk. Emma was suddenly conscious of her own flimsy nightie, but Nicholas didn't seem to notice. The only emotion that altered his severity was one of undoubted surprise.

Emma explained about the dressing table and Nicholas nodded his agreement, coming right into the room now and standing awkwardly on the rug in front of the fireplace.

'I was down at the lodge earlier today,' he began slowly. 'Apparently they're left with a couple

of pups. They think one's sold – but the other is
no good for showing,' he shrugged, 'feet too long
or something, they're bound to have trouble getting rid of it.' He paused, and his eyes almost
crackled as they ran her quickly up and down.
Emma's heart lurched at his obvious attraction,
but then the look was gone, his face almost im-
passive, as he asked mildly, 'Would you like it –
the puppy? It seems a fetching little thing.'

Emma stared at him in astonishment. 'You
can't be serious,' she stammered. 'A puppy ...
just think ...'

'It will be your responsibility, of course,' he
was taking the firm line again. 'It's your birthday
some time next week, isn't it? It can be your
present.' He didn't look at her again as he strolled
over to the door. 'I said you'd let them know tomorrow. I'll leave it up to you, then, okay?'

Emma nodded, and he left. Then the smile
slowly slipped from her face. She felt lost, alone
and unloved. Silly. She slid back between the
sheets, thinking of the puppy, of the joy she had
felt that Nicholas had remembered her birthday.
But why couldn't he have kept it for a surprise?
Then it would have been a real birthday treat. He
had made it sound so casual – so unimportant.
Emma turned off the light and snuggled down.
But at least she didn't have to wait until next
Sunday. She could have the puppy tomorrow. It

would be nice to have something to cuddle.

The little spaniel puppy was indeed very cuddly; the next morning everyone declared this was the case. It was also a great time-waster, and when the two cookery students were preparing the dining room for lunch, Emma was crouching beside its bed, tickling its tummy, and having her finger gently nibbled.

'What's its name?' Nicholas had come softly into the kitchen and Emma jumped at the sudden sound of his voice.

'It isn't an *it* – it's a her,' she said, picking up the warm bundle of trouble for his inspection. 'Her name's Piety – for devotion.'

With the squirming bundle of mischief in his arms, Nicholas didn't seem very impressed.

'I shall call you Pixie,' he announced to the tiny creature; then his taunting expression dared Emma to question it.

Her face flushed at the memory of the pet name he used to call her.

'You can't,' she said emphatically. 'Her name's Piety – it's on her pedigree ...'

He dismissed the authority of the Kennel Club with a disdainful shrug. 'I don't care,' he said. 'I shall call her Pixie.' He did – and the name stuck!

CHAPTER NINE

SUNLIGHT streamed through the crack between Emma's bedroom curtains. She stretched and smiled to herself, wondering why she felt just a little bit excited. Then the smile broadened and her toes curled as she remembered it was her birthday.

Twenty-three! She looked at her outstretched hands to see if there were any signs of age upon them. Not yet. Then the smile faded as her eyes gazed at the plain gold wedding ring. Its brightness mocked her – as did the simple gold and emerald pendant, every time she ran upstairs and looked at the portrait.

Gail Weston – the name came back to haunt her again. She saw the blonde woman's cool sophistication, the assured and natural rapport she had with Nicholas. Of course they couldn't marry – perhaps that was their tragedy. Or was it? Couldn't they have simply lived together? Couldn't Nicholas have persuaded the woman he loved to forfeit a king's ransom? His powers of persuasion were excellent. Hadn't he used them on the Trustees and won a free hand with Whitewayes for a year?

Emma frowned, and began sitting up in bed. Yet, if his powers of persuasion were that good, why hadn't he persuaded the Board to let Emma remain on in her capacity as assistant. Why give in to their ageing moral values so readily? Wasn't his method of gaining their approval somewhat drastic and quite out of character? Nicholas Voss didn't normally dance to anyone else's tune.

The alarm rang and she hammered it to silence. She had better look slippy, in another half an hour the girls would be arriving to prepare breakfast, the house would be pulsing to life, and Pixie was probably dying to go out.

Emma slipped on her dressing-gown and hurried down the front stairs, the smile back on her face. Blow them all! This was her birthday. She was determined to have a lovely day.

The little tan and white puppy greeted her with whimpers of delight; and Emma rushed her outside before there was an accident. The morning was fresh, the grass damp through her slippers, and she watched the puppy scampering about, feeling pleased that it had settled in so well after only a week.

Then Emma picked her up and hurried back indoors. 'I won't be long,' she said, bending and receiving an affectionate lick. 'If we're not careful we're going to spoil you,' she laughed, remembering Colin, last night, sitting with Pixie on his lap as they had discussed the day's events around the sitting room fire.

Nicholas had been smoking one of his occasional cigars, Louis had lit a pipe – the room would seem pretty stuffy this morning. Emma decided it might be a good idea to open the windows before anyone came down.

The heavy velvet curtains shut out the light, but Emma moved automatically towards the french windows, and with a flourish she spilled air and light into the room. She breathed deeply. That was better. Then she turned back towards the door ... and then she saw them!

She was rooted to the spot. Topaz eyes opened wide in amazement, she could feel her jaw drop – and her mind went numb as she tried to grasp exactly what it meant.

'One ... two ... three ...' She moved towards the table, counting, wondering if they were a mirage. But they weren't – and there were twelve of them – that made a dozen. A dozen of the most beautiful scarlet roses she had ever seen.

She tottered backwards and sat down on the arm of a chair. She couldn't take her eyes off them. No one had ever sent her roses before – gorgeous, half-opened blooms on straight green stems. And they couldn't have been delivered this morning. Not at this time – not on a Sunday.

Who could have left them there since last night?

Surely — no, surely Nicholas wouldn't have ...
Instinctively, Emma moved towards the table
again. Yes, there was a small white envelope
tucked between the blooms. Her fingers prised it
out carefully, and she noticed they were trembling a little as she extricated the smooth white card
from inside. There was a plain gold edging — the
words had been printed in gold, they said quite
simply, Happy Birthday, Emma.

And as simply as that she knew how wrong
she had been. Wrong — because of course he loved
her. Wrong — because he could persuade anyone
to do anything. He had married Emma for all the
right reasons after all. And this was his way of
telling her.

But he thinks I don't love him ... Emma was
swept along on a cloud of emotion. And now
there was no time to tell him. Soon the house
would be alive ... What could she say? How
could she explain in front of others? ... The
little clock chimed the quarter hour and Emma
held her breath. There was just fifteen minutes
more. Fifteen minutes to say I've loved you for
ever. Even before I met you ... That we belong
together ... Emma suddenly knew she had the
strength to say it all.

She plucked a rose from the arrangement and
raced back upstairs, two at a time, not noticing

the portrait with so much else on her mind.

She burst into Nicholas' room, her face glowing with joy, disbelief, and wild abandon. Nothing was going to stop her now. This was the best birthday she had ever known.

Her husband was coming out of his adjoining bathroom and he clutched together the fronts of his silk robe as he stared at her in utter bewilderment.

'Nicholas, they're beautiful,' she enthused from the doorway. 'Such a lovely thought — why didn't you say? ...' and before he was able to say anything she hurtled across the room and fell against him.

'Emma, what the ...' His arms wrapped around her, firm, yet unsure.

'Such a lovely surprise,' she smiled up at him, still holding the rose as she locked her fingers around his neck and silently pleaded for a kiss.

He looked as confused as any man could be. Almost indulgent, she thought, as if he imagined she had suddenly gone mad.

But the madness seemed to appeal to him as he gradually realised he held a warm and glowing girl in his arms. And she was smiling up at him, invitingly. It was an invitation to stir the senses of any red-blooded male. Nicholas couldn't resist, as she had known from the beginning.

Yet his kiss was brief — a mere featherlight

touch on her lips, and when she didn't disappear into thin air, he closed his eyes and gathered her firmly against him. This time his kiss was warm and strong and hinted at an almost frightening depth of emotion stored away deep within him.

This time Emma wasn't frightened; like a warm kitten she snaked seductively into him, longing to possess — to be possessed ... Excitement danced through her limbs. She felt reckless, elated, and filled with such love that it really, really hurt. This man was her husband, and oh, how she wanted him, now — this very minute.

Nicholas slowly raised his head, his eyes were tormented. 'Yes, I want you too,' he began breathlessly, and she could feel the tangle of passion buried within him.

'Well then?' she suggested, holding the rose in one hand and sliding the other one down the open front of his robe. She traced delicate circles through the soft hairs on his chest, then she spread her palm flat and felt the violent thundering of his heart.

'There isn't time, little one,' he said wretchedly. She pouted and tugged at soft silk. He laughed. 'Careful, you might get more than you bargained for!' Then his face was instantly serious and when he bent to kiss her again there was an inevitableness about it which made Emma's heart sing. Her dressing-gown belt was being pulled undone. 'You little minx, what have you done to me?' he breathed, and then they both stopped breathing as his sensuous hand eased its way inside her wrap.

It was sensational, exquisite torture, and Emma knew she was hopelessly lost as Nicholas coaxed and caressed every sensitive inch of her, until she gave a low, husky moan which seemed to be the sign he had been waiting for.

In agony, he drew away, attempting to disengage her hands which were both around his neck again. Then he flinched and frowned, and with a stab of remorse, Emma realised the rose she was still holding had scratched him.

He stared at the sweet-smelling bloom as if seeing it for the first time.

'I should have been more careful – is it bleeding?' Emma stood on tiptoe and tried to see.

'It's nothing.' He was almost brusque, then with eyes staring into nowhere he kissed her forehead and gave her bottom a pat. The light had gone out of his eyes, and worse, she could feel the warmth and passion seeping out of his body. Her own body was still alive and dancing – but something had happened. Was it just because of the scratch? She felt suddenly cold and miserable inside.

'Happy birthday, Emma.' He said the words with some ceremony. 'It's a pity it falls on such

a busy day.' His obvious dismissal hurt dreadfully, so she twiddled the long stem between her
fingers and bent to smell the delicate perfume;
the simple gesture hiding her face so that he
shouldn't see the pain. When her eyes met his
again she looked as bright and sparkling as the
April morning; how else were you supposed to
look when your husband had decided not to make
love to you?

'It must be nearly breakfast time,' she chirped,
then with a little shrug she indicated the rose and
said, 'Thanks anyway,' but he only looked at her
and said nothing.

'Emma!' She glanced back from the doorway,
feeling small and lost and wishing he would let
her go before she fell to pieces. 'I was just going
to suggest that we have breakfast together —
in the little dining room. I mean just the two of
us,' he went on awkwardly, '... as it's your birthday.'

'All right,' was all she could think of saying
after staring at him for ages. It was no good, she
would never understand him. He really was a
very bewildering man; but back in her bedroom
she put the rose under her pillow. Why? She
didn't really know. Just because ... just in case ...

If it hadn't been for the shared breakfast, a tiny
oasis of calm in the turbulent day, Emma would
have felt sad and deflated after Nicholas' abrupt

behaviour in his bedroom that morning.

Nothing exciting happened as they sat at either end of the table, and instinct told her to play the game as calmly as her husband. She felt confused by his obvious preoccupation. What had she done wrong? Had she imagined what had happened when he had held her close? Maybe he always switched from lover to businessman with the practised ease of an expert.

'Where's Prentice?' he asked, when they were gathering the bits and pieces to take back to the kitchen.

For a moment Emma was thrown off her stroke. 'Oh, *Colin*.' It sounded strange to hear him spoken of in that way. 'He's not coming in till around ten-thirty. He isn't wanted until his talk at eleven. Shall I tell him you want to see him?'

Nicholas frowned and shook his head quickly. 'Don't bother.' Then the curious expression in his eyes melted away; he smiled – then kissed her. 'Happy birthday,' he said again. Then he was gone, out into the hustle and bustle. But the day was suddenly bright again, Emma felt like dancing, yet beneath the brightness she sensed an unknown edge of tension. Was it excitement, or nerves? Was something wonderful about to happen – or something completely shattering?

Emma told herself not to be silly, but the feeling followed her around the house, as she stripped beds and prepared the laundry. Then, as it was still a lovely morning, she decided that coffee could be served in the little walled garden.

'I'll see to it,' she told the two girls who were in the middle of preparing lunch, and with Pixie to help her, Emma carried out basket chairs and small tables. The garden was sheltered, the spring flowers such a joy after the dark days of winter, and a magnolia tree was just about to burst majestically into bloom. Emma loved this garden, it was so peaceful, cloistered, with its warm, mellow brickwork and tall wrought-iron gate. It was a little spot of privacy not open to the public, but Emma didn't mind sharing it with the weekend guests. They really weren't such a bad lot. It was nice to hear them laughing and chatting in the evenings. Almost as if the house had brought back one of those social occasions from the past. People suited Whitewayes, they brought it alive in all the dark corners. And if they could help the finances, then maybe it was a good thing ...

'So this is how you spend your time, is it? Day-dreaming. Lucky for you I wasn't Nicholas.'

Emma turned suddenly, surprised as much by her train of thought as by Colin's unexpected appearance. Pixie hurtled across the grass to meet him, her tail wagging, ears flying out behind her like banners. Colin had already made another conquest.

As he came towards her carrying the puppy, she thought, yes, he should have been a farmer; so solidly dependable, so gentle and comforting. If it wasn't for Nicholas she might have made him happy ...

He came and stood beside her. 'What were you day-dreaming about?'

'Nothing much.' She shrugged, aware that he was looking at her expectantly, and wondered what it was she was supposed to say. 'Oh, Nicholas wants to see you,' she remembered suddenly, and Colin's face clouded. What was the matter? she wondered. Had the two men had a disagreement? Best to keep out of it. Let them sort it out for themselves. If Colin wanted her help he would ask for it.

'Happy birthday,' he said suddenly, stooping to kiss her forehead and getting licked by Pixie in the process.

'Thank you.' She smiled up at him brightly, knowing that he wouldn't have forgotten, but it was nice to have it confirmed. 'Let's sit down for five minutes,' she said, sinking into one of the basket chairs, and Colin pulled up one beside her.

'Did you like them?' he asked, crossing one leg over the other and dancing the puppy on his knee. 'Your birthday present,' he continued, looking at her in an old-fashioned way. 'Didn't I tell you that I'd get them for you one day? There are a dozen, you know. They're supposed to melt your heart.'

Emma's smile froze until she thought her face would crack. The sky fell in, and she saw hope and illusion washed away in despair.

'I left them at the lodge,' he said, imagining her silence to be one of admiration. 'The gardener's wife said she'd bring them in when she came up to clean through. I wanted them to be there before you came down,' he said, almost childishly. 'I wanted them to be a surprise.'

'They were.' Emma hoped her tone was right, but she didn't seem to have much control over her voice. 'It was very brave of you – to send roses to a married lady.' Of course, that was why Nicholas wanted to see Colin. What a fool she had been not to realise; to automatically jump to the conclusion she wanted to believe. Nicholas hadn't sent her the roses; hadn't used them as an excuse to tell her that he loved her. Nothing was changed – and then with a jerk she realised that everything was. Now Nicholas knew how she really felt and he had still rejected her. Humiliation swept through her like a hot flood. Somehow she had to get out of this garden – away from Colin – if only she could run and run and never stop.

'I'd better go and see about coffee, they'll be out in a minute,' she said, glancing at her watch and jumping awkwardly to her feet. 'I'm having

a special supper tonight,' she went on, turning
back to him so as not to appear quite so brisk.
'Uncle Louis' staying on – you'll come as well,
won't you?' And he smiled uncertainly, nodded,
then deposited Pixie back down on the grass.
'That's fine.' Emma's smile was slipping. 'Must
dash.' And then she was racing back to the house,
the puppy desperately trying to keep up.

The phone was ringing as she passed Nicholas'
office. It was the private line and she wondered
who could be using it.

'Dreadfully sorry to bother you,' said the
female voice on the other end, 'but I wonder if
I could possibly speak to Nicholas.'

Emma closed her eyes and sank into his chair.
It was Gail Weston. That was all she needed!

CHAPTER TEN

It didn't turn out to be the most successful of supper parties. Some demon had prompted Emma to invite Gail as well.

'Well, I won't be so outnumbered,' she had said lightly, waving a hand towards the three men as they had gathered for a sherry before the meal. And Gail had laughed, a light, silvery sound, that matched her flaxen hair and delicate aura. 'I'm glad you could come at such short notice,' Emma had continued, and that had been true, because she was glad the woman had come. Very glad. It seemed a splendid opportunity to show Nicholas that she didn't love him at all.

It had been easy to keep out of her husband's way all day. There had been an awkward moment this evening, when she had been changing for dinner. The handle of her locked bedroom door had slowly turned, and she had watched in horror as it worked silently backwards and forwards. But he hadn't called out – hadn't mentioned the fact afterwards; and now, seated at the long table, she could gaze at him undetected, as he bent towards Gail Weston and laughed seductively.

Yes, they made a good pair. How could she have ever thought differently? Although Nicholas hadn't welcomed the news of this extra guest when she had told him.

'If that's what you want,' he had said, and his blue eyes had been as unfathomable as the ocean ...

'That really was an excellent meal, my dear,' said Uncle Louis, bringing her back to the present with a start. 'It's a pity we don't have birthdays more often,' then remembering his own age he quickly retracted.

'It hasn't been very exciting for you,' said Colin with a touch of hostility, and Emma realised he was almost as confused as herself. What had possessed him to send her those flowers? She remembered some promise he had once made, about love and roses, but that was ages ago. Surely, now that she was married, all that was over. Or did Colin secretly hope ... ?

'Oh, it's been a splendid birthday, really,' she chirped, and Nicholas turned quickly from the woman at his elbow, and flashed her an ominous warning. There was something in his eyes that stirred her blood to fire. Antagonism crackled down the table between them, and suddenly all the hurt of the day welled up within her crying out for release – or was it for revenge? 'My uncle gave me some scent,' she said, looking past Louis to the woman beside him, then ignoring her husband, she slid her eyes across the table, adding, 'and Colin gave me some *gorgeous* roses ...'

'Oh, I thought ...' Gail Weston began, 'naturally I assumed ...' then she smiled in a slow, almost self-satisfied way, and turned her laughing eyes upon their host. 'And what did Nicholas give you?' she enquired mischievously. But it was exactly what Emma had hoped she would say.

'Nothing – nothing at all,' she began, from her end of the table, yet it was impossible to ignore the thin line of Nicholas' lips, his cheeks pinched tight with anger, and the dangerous light burning in his eyes.

'Maybe you've had nothing yet, my dear,' his voice trembled a little in rage, 'but believe me, you'll have your little – present – before your birthday is over.' The atmosphere froze them all to silence until Gail eventually laughed and Colin cleared his throat.

'I always get my cheese from Harrods,' Uncle Louis announced with perfect timing, and they all stared at him as he continued calmly, 'they do an excellent Stilton, but this one is superb, my dear.' And everyone was suddenly talking about grocers and cheese and Emma left them to it. Perhaps they could hire out Uncle Louis as the perfect dinner guest. She must mention it to him some day.

There wasn't time for Colin to have a few words alone with Emma, not until everyone was leaving and he led her away from the little gathering in the hall.

'You're sure you're all right?' he asked quickly, touching her arm in concern. 'You know where I am if ...'

'Don't be silly; everything's fine,' she assured him, conscious all the while that Nicholas was watching them. Then they all wandered outside, and it was Louis who was taking her hand and planting a kiss on her pale cheek.

'A very pleasant evening, my dear.' His eyes were quietly grave for once. 'You reminded me of your mother when she was your age. Such a wealth of understanding, she had, for such young shoulders.' Then he was shaking hands with Nicholas and climbing into his car, and Emma watched her uncle curiously. Why had he talked of her mother? Was he trying to suggest that Emma act with more maturity? It was all very well for him to talk like that, but neither he nor her mother had ever had to cope with Nicholas Voss. She watched the ancient Rolls purr to life, its tyres crunching on the gravel as Louis eased the car slowly forward. Then Gail was about to leave in a flash of Alfa-Romeo and Emma tried to make her escape — but Nicholas stopped her.

'Come and wave goodbye,' he said cheerfully,

slipping what looked like a loving arm around her shoulders. But his fingers bit into her flesh; it wasn't an embrace – it was a cruel, vicious trap as he pinned her against him.

Colin was the last to leave and he looked back at them both thoughtfully before his car reached the bend in the drive and he was lost from sight.

It wasn't until the front door closed behind them that Nicholas finally allowed Emma to break free.

'I'm going to put Pixie out,' she said quickly. He couldn't argue with that – and he didn't even try.

When she had settled the puppy and turned off the kitchen light, Emma discovered that the rest of the downstairs rooms had been similarly shrouded in darkness. The hall and landing lights had been left on. Had Nicholas gone up to bed without her? ... Emma hastily re-phrased that in her mind. Had Nicholas gone up to bed without saying any of the things he had bottled up all evening?

As she passed the sitting room door she heard the delicate chimes of the half-hour. Only thirty minutes left before midnight. Only thirty minutes more of her birthday. And then she remembered her husband's threat, and fear touched a heart which only that morning had glowed with love.

How long ago it all seemed – and what a fool's

paradise she had been living in. Just like this whole marriage, she reflected sadly, her feet dragging up the marble stairs until she came to a stop below the full-length portrait. Only this time, instead of seeing a dark-haired young woman in a white gown, she imagined a flaxen-haired beauty in the deep pink dress she had worn that night ... But the pendant didn't have to be imagined. It was there, before her now, and Emma wondered how long it would be before Gail Weston wore the original.

Emma could see again the gold and emerald pendant lying on black velvet, as Nicholas had shown her on that far-off day when it was still winter. 'For the mistress of Whitewayes,' he had said, but he hadn't given it to Emma — and he obviously had no intention of doing so now.

A fool's paradise! Oh, she was a fool indeed; a fool ever to have deluded herself that she could make this marriage work. *Some* arranged marriages worked, of course they did. But only as business partnerships, with maybe respect, but nothing more, on both sides. But this situation was hopeless. She loved Nicholas, and she doubted she even had his respect.

She noticed a light under his door as she crept past. It was hard to believe that she had got away with everything so easily, it wasn't like Nicholas to bluff. He usually meant everything he said.

It didn't surprise her to find the light on in her own room. She could have forgotten to turn it out when she had changed for supper, and it wasn't until she had closed her door and turned back into the room that she realised her husband was standing before her.

'I wanted to make sure that you didn't lock me out again.' Nothing had been bluff, nothing had been forgiven, and she knew that Nicholas had come to take his revenge.

It took all Emma's courage to appear calm as she crossed to her dressing table and removed her wrist-watch. She could feel Nicholas following every move she made. The measure of his gaze fell like a lance across her back. She stepped out of her shoes and the hem of her long cream dress crumpled around her toes. Only Nicholas saw how tired she looked, how very young and vulnerable. And the only appearance Emma was interested in was that of her husband. How tall and dangerous he was, seeming to fill the room and become part of the very air she breathed. His face was almost cruel as he surveyed her trembling figure with icy blue eyes.

'It's rather late – I'm very weary,' she tried to sound rational. 'I don't think this is a very good time to talk.'

'Talk!' His eyes lifted from the pulse beating in her throat. 'I haven't come here to *talk*, Emma.

I've done enough talking – enough waiting ...'
He paused, the silent seconds stretched ominously
longer, and Emma felt the blood stirring uncom-
fortably through her as she watched the muscles
in his face tighten. It was the sign that he was
holding himself in fierce check and she realised
it wouldn't take much for the storm to break.

'You really can't expect me to tolerate such
behaviour,' he said eventually. 'On our wedding
day I find you in the arms of another man – and
now this ...' his voice had increased to one of
outrage as he repeated, '*this – blatant –* flaunting
of my wishes. When I asked for a year, Emma,
I meant it. Three hundred and sixty-five days of
wifely devotion.' He laughed harshly, throwing
back his head and displaying a strong, sun-tanned
throat. 'Devotion, that's good!' His eyes devoured
her. 'You don't even know the meaning of the
word,' he accused at last.

'What do you want me to do?' she stormed,
hurt beyond caring for expedience. 'I can't help
it if people are kind – if they send me presents,'
she added, cleverly reminding him that he hadn't
done so. 'Would you like to lock me up in an
ivory tower?' What a stupid thing to say. Ivory?
Why did they have to be ivory?

'There's only one thing I'm going to do with
you,' Nicholas replied. It seemed his thoughts
weren't panicked into straying off course.

'Don't you lay one finger on me,' she challenged, 'or I'll ...'

'You'll what?' he taunted. 'Scream for help? But who'll hear you? We're alone, Emma, in this vast, echoing house ...'

'You're the one who can stay here alone,' she declared, hitching up her skirt and trying to rush past him. But she needn't have bothered. He reached out and grabbed her before she was even halfway to the door.

'You ran away from me before,' he said, and there was a wildness in his eyes she had never seen before. 'But you shan't do so again. I want you, Emma, and by God I'm going to have you. You're my *wife*!' he shouted in justification, and with all the pent-up fury of five long years.

She tried to struggle out of his grasp, to run away again, and then she was suddenly tired of running. She was furious; with herself for caring – with Nicholas for *not* caring – and with Colin for complicating everything and turning her lovely birthday into this hopeless mess.

So now she wasn't just struggling to be free; she was pushing against him, trying to hurt him, but he only laughed and fended her off easily, so she screwed up her face, took a deep breath – and kicked him.

'You little devil ...' It hurt Emma's bare toes far more than his shin, but it was just the final straw and something snapped inside them both.

Emma went berserk – arms flaying, her supple young body wriggling and squirming, her fists clenched as she hammered into any part of him she could reach.

Nicholas' face swam before her blurred vision. Her tears were of rage and frustration. Rage, because she couldn't hurt him, couldn't get through that bright, brittle exterior – and frustration because she wanted him to ...

'So you want a fight, do you? Then let me give you something to fight about,' he taunted, searching for the long zip down the back of her dress.

'Don't you dare ... you *fiend* ...'

'You can do better than that,' he mocked, dodging another blow and tugging the zipper down at least six inches. The dress fell off her shoulders, Nicholas' eyes ignited, he gave a final yank and it crumpled around her feet.

It was like one of those dreams when you find yourself walking down the high street in your underwear. Only it wasn't the high street – it was an intimate bedroom and the only person to see Emma was her husband.

In the brief second she was shocked into immobility, Nicholas picked her up and pulled back the duvet, tumbling her into bed.

Then the fight began again, only now it was exciting, her blows tempered, and his warding them off was a display of strength, and a message of what was to come.

At last he kissed her, hard and full on the mouth, as his hands swept possessively over the smoothness of her body. Her lacy bra and pants came off slowly, inch by inch, their tormenting removal gradually firing Emma with a primitive release that she had never experienced before. She was a woman – she was his wife. *Please* let him love her. And she knew he would, even though he now flung the cover wide and slowly eased himself to his feet.

Emma was hot, breathless, her condition made worse as she lay naked and uncovered with her husband staring down at her. He was suddenly very calm and she knew this was the time to run away – he wouldn't try to stop her. But she knew she didn't want to go.

He stood there for maybe a minute, her eyes trapped by his, and when she didn't speak or move he very gradually slipped off his jacket and threw it across a chair. She could see a muscle jerking in his cheek which was taut with desire. Then his hands went up to his tie and the silk swished when he finally pulled the knot undone.

It seemed an eternity, but it didn't really take him long, and soon he was snaking in beside her, covering the duvet over them both, and Emma drew her breath at the exquisite sensation of bare limbs caressing each other.

Yet mixed up in the joy of it all there was still a tang of fear. Emma discovered she was holding herself tight – frightened, in spite of herself, at the thought of what he might do.

Nicholas was immediately aware of her condition. 'It's all right, little one,' he assured gently. 'I know you've a lot to learn ...' And now he wasn't rough any more, but tender, unhurried, and Emma's fear melted away as he slowly kissed every inch of her body. He kissed her toes – no one had ever kissed her toes before – then he kissed her knees and finally, a long time afterwards, he was kissing the tips of her fingers. There wasn't anywhere at all left undiscovered.

At last it was impossible to lie there and be kissed. She touched his shoulder, her eyes conveying their silent message, and he smiled and stretched out beside her, allowing young, inexperienced hands to make shy discoveries of their own. But he couldn't stand it for long. Soon he was pulling her down on top of him and they were rolling over together, as close – nearly as close – as a man and woman could be.

In the tumble she had slipped off the pillow, now it was falling over her face, and with a little cry of impatience Nicholas tossed it carelessly to the floor. Now his gentleness was barely concealing the fierce driving force within him. There was nothing else left to do – somehow they had driven each other to the edge at exactly the same time.

Emma snaked up against him, running her fingers down the hardness of his back, her eyes momentarily closed at the sheer wonder of it all.

And then she opened her eyes and stared up at the face of the man above her. His expression had frozen, and the sight of it touched Emma's heart like an icy, bitter wind. What was the matter? What had gone wrong? And now Nicholas' lips were moving – not to smile – but to draw back tightly against gleaming white teeth. His eyes glared at her with hatred. Never had she seen him, anyone, look so desperate, so angry, hurt and bitter.

'What's the matter?' she managed to whisper at last. She had to say something – before her heart stopped entirely.

'My God, Emma, what manner of man do you take me for?' He picked up something that had been under the pillow. It was the rose, one of the birthday roses she had put there that morning. Only that was before she had realised ... And the sight of it had dragged Nicholas into a black abyss of rage.

'Colin Prentice sending my wife roses,' he muttered, almost inaudibly, and all the anger and frustrations of his day were behind the heavy tone. 'You are forgetting the rules, Emma. *No one* sends my wife roses – she does *not* keep them under her pillow – and *I* do not make love to a woman when she's been encouraging another man!'

'I haven't ...' Emma began, struggling to cover herself as he got to his feet and stared down at the bed. 'I haven't encouraged him, Nicholas. Honestly. I haven't said a word.'

'Prentice wouldn't do *anything* without encouragement.' Nicholas' face was tormented. 'So you see, Emma, I just don't believe you!'

CHAPTER ELEVEN

THE taxi was halfway to Highgate before Emma remembered that Colin didn't live there any more. The driver muttered to himself and skidded round the one-way system, setting off in another direction.

Emma sank back into the seat again, cross with herself at forgetting, yet still in a daze that she had actually had the courage to be here at all. Pixie was snuggled into her lap, oblivious of the enormous step her mistress had taken.

But it had really been the only possible thing to do. Emma closed her eyes and still couldn't believe it had all happened...Being with Nicholas, showing how very much she loved him — and having him turn on her so cruelly in the end. Her mind had been made up even as she had crawled from the bed, cold and miserable, packing a few things and creeping out of the house, managing to phone for a taxi without being heard. Whatever happened, it couldn't be so bad as coming downstairs the next morning and having to face Nicholas. What would have happened to the fine balance of their arrangement? Her pride had been blown to the wind. No one, not even Uncle Louis, would expect her to stay under those conditions.

So why wasn't she on her way to her uncle's. Perhaps it was what she ought to have done, might still do – tomorrow, when there had been time to sort everything out. But she could rely on Colin for a warm, comforting welcome – and Emma needed so desperately to be comforted.

She paid off the taxi when it stopped in front of the elegant showrooms. The name Nicholas Voss stretched across the fascia, it had been a long time since she had stood there before. The little street was deserted, the driver asked if she would be all right, and she tried to smile as she nodded and watched him drive away. Then, sighing, she picked up her case and the puppy, and carried them both round to the little mews at the back of the shops.

The second flight of wrought-iron stairs led to the flat above Nicholas' premises. It was all in darkness, but that was hardly surprising at two o'clock in the morning. Poor Colin, he would have been in bed hours ago.

He eventually came to the door, sleepy, confused, a light dressing-gown hastily pulled on over pyjamas. When he saw who it was he opened the door even wider and gazed down at her in surprise. Then he noticed her case – and the puppy in her arms – and surprise gave way to absolute amazement.

'You've left him,' he said simply and Emma nodded, bit her lip – then finally burst into tears.

Who but Colin, dear Colin, would have swept her into a comfortable chair, put the fire on, made some cocoa, found a stool for her feet and a dozen handkerchiefs to mop up the salty flood?

'It had to happen,' he soothed. 'You couldn't have gone on like that, love.' And Emma hardly noticed what he was saying, let alone the meaning of his words.

'I'll – I'll go to Uncle Louis in the morning,' she sniffed. 'I don't want to be a nuisance – but I thought you'd understand ...'

He crouched beside her chair and gently smoothed her hair into place. 'You don't have to go anywhere, Emma.' He paused and cleared his throat. 'You can stay here for as long as you like ...'

'Oh, no – I couldn't, really – it wouldn't be right.' She sipped her chocolate and stared at him with misty eyes over the top of the mug.

'I suppose you're right – this is his flat,' Colin acknowledged, and that wasn't what Emma had meant at all. She sank back and closed her eyes, having the dreadful feeling that she had run away from one hopeless mess and straight into another.

'Colin,' she said eventually, opening her eyes and looking into his which were level with her own. He was stroking her hand, but she tried not to notice. 'Colin,' she began again, 'why did you send me those roses? I mean, any flowers would have been bad enough ... But what did I say? ... What made you think? ...' She trailed to silence and watched the last shred of hope slip from his face. She felt so sorry for him – but it had to be said. Now, at last, he would really understand.

'I thought it was all pretty quick,' he said quietly. 'This marriage business. Even if you did know each other years ago.' He shrugged. 'But I suppose I thought you both knew your own minds – until ...'

'Until?' she prompted, and he pulled the other armchair near and dropped into it.

'Until we used your dressing table for my talk the other week.' He seemed rather embarrassed, and she waited for him to continue in his own time. 'It was obvious you weren't sharing a room – that you weren't sleeping together,' he said at last, and Emma felt herself blush as if it had been all her fault. 'I didn't believe it,' Colin went on, still looking a bit dazed, then his grey eyes hardened and the soft mouth welded together in anger. 'What the hell does he think he's playing at? – getting you to marry him under those conditions. You can't throw away your life on a *house*, Emma. Not even Whitewayes. Not even because

Nicholas Voss is a very persuasive man.'

'I didn't.' A tear trickled down her nose and she wiped it away angrily. 'I married Nicholas because I loved him – and I left him because I still love him.' Colin looked at her as if she was going mad. 'It's just that he doesn't love me – never has – doesn't like me much, either.' Now she had started there was no stopping her. 'He never said he did,' she explained hurriedly, when Colin looked as if he was about to explode. 'He just wanted me to stay on and help him run White-wayes. It was all me,' she confessed, 'it was me who thought that maybe one day he'd love me. Bit silly, wasn't it?' she tried to add cheerfully, but the smile cracked and slid off her face.

Colin sprang out of his chair and began pacing about the floor. 'Damned Trustees,' he swore. 'Lot of interfering old men ...'

'You know about the letter, then?' Emma felt even worse now. The letter was something she didn't really want to believe in.

Colin looked over his shoulder. 'What letter?'

'It doesn't matter,' she shrugged, 'it's a long story.'

'I suppose they didn't like the idea of you living there with him.' Emma nodded and Colin swore under his breath again. 'Your uncle was telling me they've always had married men ...'

'But my father ...' Emma reminded him.

'Maybe he was a widower, but he had you, love. I expect you were sitting at the other end of his dining table, being the perfect little hostess, and looking absolutely gorgeous,' he added softly, 'long before you even left school.'

Emma nodded again. And it had been on one of those social occasions when she had been eighteen that she had first met Nicholas. He had probably thought her very smart and sophisticated, chatting happily to perfect strangers. But it was just a knack she had acquired over the years. It hadn't made her the sophisticated woman he had imagined her to be. She still wasn't, five years later. Thinking of Gail Weston, Emma doubted she could ever reach her standard.

'You'd better try and get some sleep,' said Colin, returning from memories and hopes of his own to the harsh realities of the present. 'The spare room bed's already made up. Would you like a bottle – it might help you to drop off?'

Emma cuddled up to the hot-water bottle, listening to Pixie's snuffles and sighs issuing from her makeshift bed in a shopping basket. But she didn't sleep as well as her puppy; in fact, dawn arrived and she was sure her eyes hadn't closed at all.

At last she could hear Colin moving around in the kitchen. It was Monday morning, but still too early, she would have thought, for him to be up and about yet. Perhaps he couldn't sleep, either. Poor dear! He seemed at last to realise there would never be anything between them. A kind friend was to be valued with precious diamonds, but it wasn't enough for marriage – Nicholas had taught her that. If she had never met him perhaps she could have been happy with Colin. But it would only have been half a happiness. Comfort instead of contentment – pleasure instead of unbounding joy. But all that was lost to her now, without Nicholas; yet she still hoped Colin would find someone who would make him really sparkle.

The door bell rang and Emma rolled over. At six o'clock in the morning! Colin was talking to someone, she couldn't hear the words, just the flat monotone of his voice as he showed the newcomer into the living room. And then there was no doubting the visitor's identity, or the absolute determination in his voice as he said, 'I've come to collect my wife!'

Emma held her breath in horror, then she was struggling up, groping for a cardigan to slip round her shoulders, but she was too late; the bedroom door burst open.

'You'd better get dressed quickly – my car is blocking the mews!' Exhaustion lined Nicholas' face; he was still wearing last night's dinner suit. Emma realised with horror that he hadn't been to bed at all.

'Nicholas, there's no point.' She shrank against the wall and this seemed to annoy him all the more.

'There's every point, my girl, because *I* tell you to. What the hell do you think you're up to anyway – coming here – spending the night with another man? ...'

'I say, look here ...' Colin had been hovering by the door; now he came inside, looking as tired and weary as his employer, but gentler, more vulnerable, and Emma instantly felt for him.

'It's all right, Colin.'

'You don't have to assure Prentice of anything,' Nicholas almost shouted. '*I'm* the one you have to assure,' he reminded her, '*I'm* your husband!'

'Husband?' Colin exploded, but a flash from piercing blue eyes stopped him from going further.

'And as your husband, I'm *telling* you to get up and get dressed. I'll give you ten minutes,' Nicholas added severely. 'If you don't want to, don't bother – I'm perfectly prepared to drive you back to Whitewayes in your nightgown.'

She had a vision of him doing exactly that! This was getting more dreadful by the moment. What could she do? If only she could think of some way ...

'Perhaps we could all do with a nice cup of tea.'

Colin was making a very big effort, she could tell.

'Good idea!' Nicholas waited for him to leave, then he closed the door and stood on guard, glaring at Emma who was still sitting up in bed. 'Come on,' he said impatiently. 'I said ten minutes – hadn't you better be making a move?'

'No!' At last Emma had just about had enough. 'I'm not getting dressed because I'm not coming with you.' Her heart thumped in terror. 'There's no point, Nicholas. I don't see why you even want me.' Each stared at the other; Emma vaguely conscious that she was offering him a final chance, while Nicholas seemed to be searching her soul for the truth.

He didn't take the opportunity she gave him, instead his mouth firmed as he glanced down at his watch. 'Now you only have five minutes left.'

'I'm not going,' Emma repeated stubbornly.

'Surely you don't still imagine yourself in love with the fellow,' he accused.

Her eyes flew to his face. 'I'm very fond ...' she began.

'Fond? Hah! *Four* minutes!'

'Get out of here – go on!' Emma shouted. Oh, the man was impossible! How could she ever have imagined herself in love with him? Maybe she would be better off with Colin – he wouldn't torment her like this.

'Three minutes. Emma, I'm warning you. I'm

very tired. I've just about had enough of this childish behaviour ...' And that was the worst thing he could possibly have said.

'Then it's a pity you didn't marry Mrs. Weston,' Emma finally exploded. 'She's certainly no child. You wouldn't have had any problems there.' She clutched the bedclothes higher, as if they could possibly form any protection. 'But couldn't you persuade her to part with all her money? Does she prefer symbols of wealth instead of love? How unfortunate you are, Nicholas, in your choice of women!' The relief of getting it all off her chest was incredible. But had she really said it? – well, practically *shouted* it ... She stared at her husband in horror. What would he do now? *No way* was he going to stand for that kind of treatment!

And he wasn't. Nicholas strode towards the bed, the enormity of her denouncement evident by the shock registered on his face.

'You've run out of time,' he said, pronouncing it like an admission of murder. Emma tried to scream, but no sound came as he reached down and dragged her out of bed. 'I'm taking you home – *now*,' he announced with authority, and suddenly Emma was being wrapped up in the eiderdown and flung over his shoulder.

'We shan't be staying for tea,' Nicholas informed the startled Colin when they all met in the passageway.

'Nicholas Voss, put me down this minute or I'll ...' Emma was red in the face with indignation. The eiderdown was a virtual straitjacket. She was as helpless as a sack of potatoes.

Nicholas paid not the slightest heed to her threat, or to the fact that she was wriggling and squirming furiously.

'I'll come back in a minute to collect her things,' he went on coolly, opening the front door and carrying her out into the chilly morning air. And what was more, Emma fumed to herself, Colin let him!

Nicholas bundled her into the front passenger seat. 'Don't move!' he glared fiercely. 'If you try to make trouble I'll say you're insane — that you've run away from hospital — and that I'm your doctor ...'

'I must have been insane to marry you!' Emma shouted, when he had slammed the door, but his only reply to that was to lock it.

'You know an awful lot about Mrs. Weston's business affairs,' Nicholas began ominously, when he had collected her gear, and the puppy, and they were finally pulling out of the mews. Emma had expected Colin to finally come to her defence, but he hadn't. He would be opening up the shop as usual, Nicholas had said, looking at her carefully as he had done so. No, Emma smiled sadly to herself, there was to be no grand gesture on her behalf, after all.

'Where did you get your information?' Nicholas persisted. 'Who told you that Gail's money is tied up in a family business?'

Emma shrugged inside her feather cocoon, her bare toes poking out at the bottom. 'Things like that are common knowledge . . . a lot of things are common knowledge . . .'

'Such as?' he enquired dangerously, turning into Piccadilly.

Emma hesitated, then, as he appeared to be concentrating on his driving she went on bravely. 'Such as her not being able to marry anyone – you,' she added forcefully, 'without losing it all.'

Nicholas drove on for several moments until her words finally sank in. 'You think I want to marry Gail, that *she* wants to marry me!' he exclaimed, screeching to a halt on double yellow lines. A heavy vehicle blew its horn and rattled past them. 'If that was what we wanted we could have lived together.' He was almost laughing at her naïveté. 'Haven't you heard, Emma, that this is the permissive age?'

'But the Trustees wouldn't have liked that either, would they?' she reminded him quickly. 'And the one thing you were determined to have – regardless of any woman – was Whitewayes.' There, that was telling him. She felt almost smug.

'What the hell do the Trustees have to do with anything ... ?' Then he broke off, remembering, and Emma met his eyes with a victorious gleam. That was the first time she had ever won a round against him.

'And you were equally determined that I shouldn't have Whitewayes, weren't you, Emma?' Now it was his turn to remind her. 'That's why you married me, wasn't it. To keep your eye on me – to stop me running riot, I think you once said ...'

Had she? All that seemed a long time ago. But what a good thing she could still use it as an excuse.

'That's right,' she said quietly, and he turned from her, crunched into gear and drove off.

It wasn't even eight o'clock when Nicholas parked right beside the front door at Whitewayes. No one saw Emma decline his assistance and hobble painfully over the gravel in her bare feet. She waited for him to bring in her bits and pieces, she let the eiderdown fall as she clutched Pixie, but the hall was chilly and she couldn't suppress a shiver.

'You'd better have a bath – warm yourself up,' Nicholas said as if he was expecting more trouble, but she nodded and made for the stairs, only the marble was even colder – her toes felt blue.

Nicholas was locking up behind him and she

went ahead; one slim, dark-haired girl in a long white nightie, utterly weary, hardly even knowing what she was doing here, except that she didn't think Nicholas was very much in love with Gail – not that it altered anything really. He still didn't love her.

Emma paused automatically beneath the portrait and gazed up at her ancestor, another dark-haired young woman in a long white dress, only she was wearing a pendant as well, a gold and emerald pendant that glistened from the artist's strokes of sunlight.

'How did you cope with it all?' Emma asked her in a tiny voice, wondering how many times the first Mrs. Voss had wearily dragged her feet upstairs. But no answer came, it never did. Answers had to be worked out for themselves.

Emma soaked in a bath for a long time. Nicholas had organised Pixie, and now she could hear him pottering about back upstairs. He seemed much more calm now that they were away from Colin's flat. Yes, it had been a mistake to go there – and it was a mistake to come back here. Now that Nicholas was in a more reasonable frame of mind perhaps she would be able to explain. Thank heaven it was Monday and they had the place to themselves.

Almost numb with tiredness and strain, Emma heaved herself out of the bath, dried quickly and slipped on her dressing-gown. She threw her nightie into the washing basket and wandered back to her room.

The curtains had been drawn against the sunlight and the room was pleasantly diffused. The electric blanket had been switched on, the bed cover pulled back. It looked very inviting, but Emma turned away.

'You look extremely tired, you ought to get some sleep,' said Nicholas from the doorway; then he came into the room looking everywhere except at her.

'I'm not staying,' she said gently. Why gently? Yet there was something about his manner that made more fighting impossible. Now that the decision had been made, now she knew she was going away, there was no need to rush. She felt almost calm. This would probably be the last conversation they would have together. Afterwards, she wouldn't like to remember there had been no attempt at compassion.

He leaned against the carved mantelpiece and put his hands into his pockets. She noticed he had changed into casual trousers and a light sweater. His hair was damp and he had shaved. The ravages of the night were less marked, except for his eyes which had lost their blue and seem grey and haunting.

'I thought we agreed on a year,' he said eventually, his voice as careful as her own had been.

'It was harder than I thought. I tried, Nicholas, really ...'

'Poor Emma. You only think you're in love, you know. But it will get easier – believe me, I know.'

Emma felt as if the last shred of camouflage had been torn from her. Naturally, after last night, he would know she loved him. Suddenly there was nothing left but to tell him the truth.

'But at least you'll understand why I can't possibly stay ...'

He nodded. 'I wouldn't have asked you to marry me if I'd realised your emotions were so deeply involved. I had no idea, Emma.'

'Why should you? Five years is a long time.'

He frowned. 'Yes. I suppose I was a bit out of touch. Louis never mentioned it.'

Emma tried to laugh. It was rather amusing to imagine Louis telling Nicholas that the bride loved the bridegroom.

'Where will you go?' His voice was hollow.

'I haven't decided.'

'There isn't anything I can say to make you change your mind?'

'You can tell me it's all been a big mistake,' she would have liked to say. 'Tell me you love me.' But the words didn't come. She had to leave here with some respect still intact.

'No,' she said instead, 'there's nothing you can say. Maybe the house is cursed after all.' He looked puzzled and she went on, 'The girl in the portrait on the landing – our great-great-grand-mother, or whoever she was, she was unlucky in love as well.'

Nicholas looked a little bemused. 'Good lord, you're right. She was married to one man and in love with another.'

'A lot of people are,' she said. 'But I wonder how many women wish it was the other way round.'

He smiled. 'What do you mean – what other way round?'

Emma wished she had never mentioned the portrait. 'I wonder how many wives wish it was their husbands that loved them, instead of the other man. Where's my suitcase?' she added, looking round the tidy room. 'I thought you brought it up.'

'It's in the wardrobe,' he said, staring fixedly at the wallpaper beside her bed.

'You've unpacked it,' she said, swinging it easily on to a low chest. But still he didn't move or utter a single comment.

Emma left him alone as she began gathering her clothes together again. Really, men were the limit, now she would have to start all over again.

'Did you put that rose under your pillow when

you thought they were from me?' he whispered, still staring at the wall.

'Of course,' she sighed, fitting in underwear in odd corners.

'Were you very disappointed when you dis-covered I hadn't sent them?' he tried again.

'Of course.' What was the matter with him? Why did he want everything spelled out?

'Emma!' At long last their eyes met. 'Emma,' he said again, 'do you – by any chance – happen to love me?'

She looked as bewildered as he, then she smiled, nodded, and whispered, 'Yes.'

'Then why ever didn't you say so?' He ran distraught fingers through his hair. 'Emma, I've been up all night. Out of my mind with worry – thinking I'd rushed you – believing you still loved Colin.'

She flopped down on the edge of her bed. 'Colin? I don't love Colin. It's you I love – always have.' She spread her hands in a little gesture of despair. 'I thought you knew – I thought that's what *you* were talking about.'

'Emma darling, what have we been doing to each other?' He held out his arms and she glided into them. He held her firm, safe, they didn't move for a long time. And Emma just let it all happen in a foggy cloud of disbelief.

'I don't understand,' she tried to say, when he

had released her sufficiently for them both to look
at each other. His eyes were blue again, tired, bemused, and shining with happiness. 'You can't be
in love with me,' she tried again. 'You never said
you were. You only married me to help you run
Whitewayes.'

For a second all expression left his face, then
it was back again, smiling, but she noticed the
momentary break in communication. 'I married
you, little one, for no better reason than that of
loving you. I'm not likely to be pushed into such
an undertaking – not by anyone. You're *sure*
you're not in love with Colin Prentice?' he added,
still in a daze.

'You're sure you're not in love with Gail
Weston,' she smiled up at him, and they both
laughed and clung together.

'Are you as tired as I am?' he asked, kissing the
end of her nose, and she nodded. 'Good.' He
smoothed a lock of her hair into place. 'Then
we'd better go to bed.'

It was a long time later when Emma finally
woke up in Nicholas' bedroom. The curtains were
still drawn against the sunshine, she could hear
birds singing, it was probably some time in the
afternoon. Slowly, so as not to disturb him, she
raised herself on one elbow and gazed down at
his face. Never had he seemed so much at peace.
A warm glow brought a smile to her lips. Her

husband! She could say the word with truth now. What warmth they had discovered together – what joy. How tenderly he had shown her the way to love.

She shifted on to her other elbow and he opened his eyes. Bright blue eyes, clear, sparkling, but the rest of his face was relaxed with contentment.

'Did I disturb you?' She was all contrite.

He shook his head. 'Come here,' he purred, pulling her gently down on to his shoulder.

Emma gasped at the sheer deliciousness of naked bodies entwined, but instead of cuddling her, Nicholas was suddenly sitting up, pulling her with him and reaching into his bedside table for a small package.

'Happy birthday,' he said, kissing her on the tip of her nose.

She stared at it in her hands. 'Is it?' she began.

'Open it and see.' And of course it was, a beautiful pendant, emerald and gold filigree, its worth far more precious than gems. 'I've been waiting a long time to give it to you, darling ...'

'Have you?'

He nodded. 'Five years is a very long time, isn't it, Emma?' and now it was her turn to nod. He kissed her and they snuggled down again.

But there was still one little problem running around in her head.

'Nicholas,' she began carefully.

'Yes, darling?' He seemed to sense something was coming.

She climbed on to her elbow again, and he looked up at her, waiting. 'Nicholas,' she repeated, 'that letter – the one from the Trustees – the one I didn't see ...' She hesitated and he waited for her patiently. 'Did they actually *say* I couldn't stay here unless we were married? In fact, was there – was there really any such letter at all?'

The silence in the room stretched on and on. The only sound came from the birds singing outside. Neither of them moved; one contemplating an answer – the other waiting for it to be given.

At last the answer came, but not in the manner she had expected.

Nicholas simply smiled, slowly, conspiratorially, until his nose wrinkled. It was all the answer Emma needed to know.

What the press says about Harlequin romance fiction...

"When it comes to romantic novels...
Harlequin is the indisputable king."
— *New York Times*

"...exciting escapism, easy reading, interesting
characters and, always, a happy ending....
They are hard to put down."
— *Transcript-Telegram*, Holyoke (Mass.)

"...always...an upbeat, happy ending."
— *San Francisco Chronicle*

"...a work of art."
— *Globe & Mail*, Toronto

"Nothing quite like it has happened since
Gone With the Wind..."
— *Los Angeles Times*